C000310973

BLURB

Obsession.
It's a sickness she brought upon me.
And I'm about to make her pay.

I shouldn't bring her into my world. But it was my father's wish, it was the ultimate revenge on our enemies.
A poised, pristine princess, too pure for this life. And me, I'm the dark prince forced to be a King too soon.

She dances gracefully, capturing my attention, before fighting me like a savage tigress. She's fire, burning through my darkness, and I'm the ice that will bring her to her knees.
Right where I like her.

I will make her bow.
I will make her submit.
And when I do, she'll be my Queen.

PLAYLIST

Guys My Age - Hey Violet

Sinner & Saint - Tommee Profitt

Bang Bang - BELLSAINT

Church - Chase Atlantic

See You Bleed - Ramsey

Scars - Boy Epic

Kill Me Slowly - Sickick

Hurt Me Harder - Zolita

9 Crimes - Damien Rice

Holy - Zolita

Monster - PVRIS

Shameless - Sofa Karlberg

Find the playlist on Spotify

WARNING

Please note, this is a dark romance which includes scenes that may trigger certain readers. If you're sensitive to dark subjects, please be wary.

Thank you!

DEDICATION

To my babes who love an unapologetic anti-hero
who likes to play with knives…

*"I don't care if I fall in love with a devil,
as long as that devil will love me
the way he loves hell."*

ENZO

My life changed two days after my thirtieth birthday.

I am a man hellbent on revenge.

Stalking down the long hallway, I button my suit jacket as I make my way toward the theater. New York is a city reveling in its nightlife, calling to those souls who need something more out of their existence. My family runs every theater in this city, and as we continue to purchase venues across the world. I know I'll have my revenge soon enough.

With a smile, I slide through the open doors and settle in the dark booth reserved for me. Mario, my right-hand man, joins me moments later. The seats are packed to capacity, and everyone is waiting with bated breath for the star of the show to appear.

"Are you sure about this?" Mario has been my conscience ever since I can remember. From the moment I was sworn into the clan—with blood dripping from my palm—to this day as I glare at the stage, he's been by my side.

I was thrown into the world my father ruled, in a city filled with Made men and violence. Where bloodshed was the order of the day and cutting someone's fingers off at sixteen was normal. This world is made up of three things that will always make more sense to me than living an ordinary life.

Money speaks loudly.

Threats are given with a smile.

And life is as fragile as a thousand-dollar crystal flute.

"Yes." My voice is cold as the word that drips poison escapes my lips.

The lights dim, the spotlight is on the blood red curtains as the gentle tinkling of classical music fills the room. Every nerve in my body sparks to life, my spine straightens, and my shoulders are tense, as I prepare for what I'm about to witness.

When the crimson drapes slide open, silence hangs heavily as we wait. The male dancer prances onto the stage dressed in black. He's the heathen in the show, the tormentor. I smile as I watch him move with grace and elegance, but it's moments later that my breath catches as I see her.

2

This isn't the first time I have watched her dance. Time and again, show after show, I've been in the darkness, a shadow in her life.

Mario leans in close, his voice a mere whisper, "It needs to happen tonight."

He's right. I know he is.

She's poised and elegant, moving across the stage like a queen. The corner of my mouth tips upward slightly as I take in her long legs, her slight curves, her tits that are bigger than most of the other dancers.

She's built for so much more than dancing, like taking my cock until she's crying. But she's born to grace the stage with her beauty. As much as I hate her, I can't deny my cock loves her.

"Do it." The two words are an order and Mario moves before I can say anything more because he knows that this is a matter of life and death. Not mine. But my pretty little dancer. He's gone before the next twirl of her small frame.

I sit back and relax, enjoying the rest of the ballet as my mind replays what happened three years ago. A nightmare. The moment I knew I would take over from my father and ensure the De Rossi name is feared in every part of this city, as well as by every Familia that attempts to cross us.

Something is wrong.

Terribly fucking wrong.

At thirty, I haven't yet found my passion. Even though I have a slew of men who would die for me, and I love my parents, there's nothing more in my life that fills me with fire. And as I pull up to the house that I've called a home for most of my life, the twisting in my gut has me on edge.

My intuition has always been strong. When I have a bad feeling, I know I need to listen to it. The moment the engine purrs up the drive, and I come to a stop outside the ornate wooden doors of the De Rossi mansion, my stomach drops.

I'm out of the car within seconds. As I step onto the gravel of our driveway, the familiar scent of New York greets me. Our home is just outside the city, overlooking the bright lights of the Big Apple. I've missed it. Even though Sicily had welcomed me with open arms, New York is in my heart. I buttoned my suit jacket as I saunter up the steps which leads to our front door.

By the time I reach the entrance, I find two of my father's men standing near the office door. My father's sanctuary, which will soon be my own, has always been a place I have always felt at peace. The soft lighting with dark wood called to me from a young age. Father would allow me to sit in an armchair and I would read while he worked.

I overheard conversations no child should, knowing that one day I would have to be the cold, ruthless killer my father was. It was only later in life that I learned that Salvatore De Rossi never got his hands dirty. He had men for that.

I on the other hand, love it.

The slippery crimson fluid on my hands has brought me a constant feeling of satisfaction. I don't just kill anyone either. I ensure they deserve it. And the more deserving, the better. I allow my sadistic side to shine through while I slice flesh from bone.

"What's going on?" I ask my father's confidante, Valentino, when I step into the office. The older man looks up as I walk in, but stays silent. It is my duty to know what's happened since I'm the Underboss, the second in command, but as I near the heavy oak desk, I realize that whatever has happened is bad. Very fucking bad.

For a long while, Valentino doesn't respond. The silence hangs heavily with foreboding. He doesn't need to speak because even before he utters the words, I know what he's about to say. That intuition I've trusted all my life burns me from the inside with the truth about what I've walked into.

The stench is obvious the deeper I move into the room. I stop at the armchair I've claimed as mine, my hand gripping the backrest as my fingers dig into the leather. A smell I know so well permeates the air. Moments pass as I breathe in the scent of death.

Valentino steps aside and my head spins with the sight before me. My eyes lock on the sight and my stomach rolls as the acid rises to my throat. I swallow back the lump in my throat, and my nails rip at the smooth fabric of my favorite chair.

"Who was it?" I don't recognize my voice as rage takes over. My heart thuds against my ribs in a painful rhythm of torture as I take in the horror. A sigh from Valentino causes me to snap my gaze to his, and once again, I grit through clenched teeth, "Who the fuck was it?"

I hear footsteps behind me, but I don't turn. I can't look away from my dead parents behind my father's desk. Salvatore sitting in his enormous black leather office chair, with my mother sitting on his lap as if they were sharing a joke.

Only, they're both bleeding from multiple stab wounds. There's so much blood, my mother's blouse is stained deep red, and my father's crisp linen shirt is nothing more than ribbons from the blade. They've used a blade, a knife, my weapon of choice for completing my jobs. This feels as if it's personal.

The sight before me blurs.

My lungs struggle to pull in air.

"We have reason to believe it was the Cavallone clan," Valentino finally speaks. He has worked for my father since they were both teens. Dad took over from his father when he was only nineteen. And now, at fifty, he's nothing more than a corpse.

"I want every man on this," I tell Valentino. "I want

to know all there is to know about the Cavallone family. I don't care how long it takes."

Realization takes hold of me as Mario's hand lands on my shoulder. My best friend. My confidante.

I will now have to step into my father's shoes and run the business. I already know the basics, how to read the books and deal with money. He said I would be ready for the upcoming challenges I may face. But this is too soon. It should've been years from now.

I graduated from Columbia with honors. But being top of my class was irrelevant right now.

Nothing could have prepared me for this.

Not any of the classes I attended. Not any of the parties I frequented.

My father stood watching the day I collected my degree. I don't know if he smiled in that moment, or if he even applauded my achievement. The black suits that surrounded him ensured he was hidden away.

Everyone in New York knew who Salvatore de Rossi was.

And everyone stood at least a few meters from where he stood.

They gave him wide berth, for good reason.

And now, I stand before him, and I must find it in my heart to say goodbye.

Valentino motions to the soldiers, who enter the room and stop on either side of the desk. Guards stand vigilant, but they don't speak. The air is heavy with sadness. I can feel their eyes on me, and even if they want to sympathize, they don't. I am the Underboss, and that position commands respect.

I take a step closer, needing to see, needing to burn the image into my mind because when I get my revenge, this is what I will remember. Valentino joins me, and Mario flanks my left.

"What is that?" I ask, gesturing with my chin toward the desk where my father's hand has been positioned perfectly, holding a piece of paper.

"We moved nothing, so I'm not sure," Valentino answers and I reach for it, tugging it from Father's fingers. The rest of him doesn't move, and my stomach rolls at the sight.

I allow my eyes to scan the piece of paper, a letter of sorts. My father's scrawl is jagged, as if he truly was afraid. Or in so much pain, he couldn't focus on holding a pen.

I did something bad a long time ago. Something I shouldn't have done. When you seek revenge, remember to do it with a clear head. Don't rush. Never run into a burning building without a plan on how to get out. I'm sorry, figlio, I've failed you in life, but I hope I can make it right in death.

In my safe is everything you need.

Frustration ebbs through me as my muscles tighten

with anxiety and I race to the safe hidden behind a painting. I don't know how my father came to have the note in his hand when he was killed, but I believe whoever murdered him didn't realize it was there.

The lock combination is one I remember as if it were my blood type. And soon, the heavy metal door swings open. Inside is cash, a lot of it, but that's not what I'm looking for. The dark blue folder with our family crest sits front and center. The silver emblem shimmering as I pick it up and bring it out.

On the first page in the folder is a contract. An arranged marriage in the event of my father's death. It makes no sense. He's always told me I'm able to do my own thing. That I didn't need to marry anyone I didn't want to.

Contratto in Morte

The three words hit me right in the chest, slamming into me like a fist from my worst enemy.

I don't turn to face anyone else because I can't come to terms with what I've just found. I'm poised to race out of this room and find the bastard and annihilate him. I still have no clear indication of what happened, but my blood burns hot as it runs through my veins.

That's what mother used to tell me; I was a bomb waiting to explode. I take after my father. We can most certainly keep our cool, but if someone comes after our Familia, our blood, that's when you see our true colors.

"Bring the men into the dining room. I want a

meeting while you clean up and sort this out." My voice is ice, cooling each syllable as I voice it. My tongue tingling with the need to throw out curses, but Father taught me a long time ago, swear words don't have people cowering in fear. Don't tell them about your anger. Show them. And I've always lived by that rule. His advice has never steered me wrong.

Valentino sighs because he knows what's coming. "Yes, sir." The respect in his response is clear. Even though I'm not yet his boss, he must obey my order. The chair behind me creaks, which means both the soldiers who walked into the office earlier have started their work.

Silently, I turn my watchful gaze on Mario, and he offers me a nod. The office is gloomy as the sun sets and the heavy velvet curtains the color of a stormy sky at dusk hang over the windows, cutting out any remaining light from outside.

I take in the space, knowing that it may be the last time I ever stand in here. I won't work in a room where my parents were murdered. Not yet, not for a long time. The dark wood paneling lines the walls, and in between are enormous works of art depicting wars and violence.

It's our lives. It's our legacy.

Death and destruction.

I move quietly on the plush carpet underfoot, which hinders the sounds of footfalls, and as I make my way through the rest of the house. I feel them before I see them. Three of the capos who work for us follow behind me and

10

stop when I settle in at the head of a twelve-seater table in the family dining room.

I wave my hand the same way my father always used to, and they each take their seats. They watch me as if I were a rabid dog. I want to smile. As if they could keep me down. Every one of them fears me, respects me, and will obey me. If my father was here, he would have the final say. But it's time for me to give the orders.

"Tell me," I say, once every chair is filled. "Who at this table will fight with me to avenge my father's death?" My question is direct. There is no time for bullshit because from what I read in the contract; I don't have a choice but to fulfill my father's dying wish for me.

Even if it is not something I want for myself.

"What happened today needs to be fixed." They all know what I mean. I know that each man at this table will want retribution for what we just witnessed. Leaning back against the backrest of my chair, I track my gaze over the faces of the men I now rule.

There will be no fanfare, no celebration, because the circumstances call for something more drastic. The weight of what happened is clear in each expression I meet. And then, without words, they each set their weapons on the table.

The first one to say something is Mario, who sits on my right. "I will stand beside you, take a bullet for you. There is no question. My weapon is your weapon." He meets my gaze, the look in his eye flickers with confidence

11

as he recites our oath, "Death before dishonor."

And in chorus, the rest of the room mimics Mario's words.

With a nod, I push back my chair and rise. After buttoning my suit jacket, I say, "I will call a formal meeting in a couple of days, and we will take action." One by one, they offer me a nod before leaving, and soon, it's only me, Mario, and Valentino. I meet the older man's stare. "Did my father tell you of this contract?"

"Yes, sir," he responds quickly. "The Cavallone clan were our enemies long before the war started here in New York. The fight was between your father and hers." His voice may be clear, but there's a hint of sadness in his words. I wonder how many of my father's secrets will die with this man.

Confusion furrows my brows as I take him in. "If he hated Mattea so much, why ensure I marry her?"

"Your father was a man who enjoyed making his enemies pay," Valentino starts. "There's a certain synchronicity to what he did. He knew one day you'd take over, and to ensure you weren't stepping into a fight, he wanted to take down his biggest enemy."

"So, in order for me to start my reign, I'm to marry this..." I wave my hand in the air with frustration. "Fifteen-year-old girl?"

"She will be eighteen in three years, so you will wait until then," he informs me, but continues quickly, "she's grown up in this life. She's not like any other girl out *there, Enzo." There's a foreboding in his tone, a warning that I shouldn't judge her before knowing her. "The principessa is the perfect wife to become your queen. And the Cavallone line will die once she takes your last name."*

There's no need for him to say anything more. We all know what will happen. We will kill them all once I'm wed to the girl.

I will kill them all.

Just then, the door bursts open and begging and pleading echoes from behind me. My movements are slow when I turn to regard the interruption with interest. It's a woman I recognize from one of our favorite restaurants in the city. One of the capos, Nico, the oldest of the three who runs guns for us, owns the pizzeria. And the woman who's being dragged into the room is one of the cooks who works in the kitchen.

"P-p-please?" she begs, and I push to my feet before Mario has time to react. I close the distance between us and stop inches from her. She tips her head back, her wide, watery eyes land on mine. "P-p-per favore?"

I nod. "Speak."

"T-they… T-t-the guns," she stutters, handing a piece of paper to me which looks like it's seen better days, but I take it, and unfold the creases. Even though she's dropped tears on the writing, it's easy to make out just who this came from.

This war has taken far too many lives. Questa

è la fine.

This is the end—the final words, written in our mother tongue.

"Cazzo!" Rage drips from my voice, poison injected into every letter that escapes my lips. "I will kill the whole fucking clan!" The Cavallone will pay, and I'll ensure every one of them meets their maker soon enough.

"Enzo, calmati." Mario is beside me. His hand on my shoulder. He's the only person who would be brave enough to even venture close to me when I'm in this mood. He's a good man and his voice calms me somewhat. But not enough to ensure my rage will be fully sated until I have blood on my hands.

Valentino takes the small note from me and curses under his breath.

"Out! Everyone out!" My order is harsh, but I grip Valentino's and Mario's arms before they can leave. Once we're alone, I turn to both men. "I may not want this woman in my life, but it was my father's last wish, and I will do as he has asked, but make no mistake, once her uncle signs the contract, they all die." My voice is rough, my throat scraping as I consider what's about to happen. "Call the men, set up the meeting, and then call Cavallone. Tell him his brother's death was not in vain."

"An eye for an eye?" Valentino asks.

My father killed the Cavallone capo, which is why they came for him. He knew what would happen. My father inadvertently killed himself by doing so, but he took my mother with him.

"There will be blood," I affirm with a nod, and he leaves to do as I asked.

Nobody will touch us. We have law enforcement in our pockets, which means nothing happens in this city and around the bordering towns without us knowing about it. It means we're able to wage war and walk away with no issue.

I think back to the book that lies in wait in my father's office, the Familia records. The last entry hasn't been filled yet, a small blank box for my name. Beside it will be the name of my future wife, also empty for now.

Mario sighs beside me. "I know you're angry, but think on it, Enzo."

Of course, I'm angry. My father wants me to marry the girl whose father and uncle are responsible for his death. He must have been out of his fucking mind.

But I cannot refuse.

My best friend watches me. For a man who just found out his parents were murdered, I'm sure I'm a picture of calmness and tranquility. My emotions only show in my dark eyes that match my father's.

"We will plan this attack, this takedown, like the professionals we are. We could rush into this tonight, but we'd lose more, and I'm not prepared to do that."

If I truly sit back and consider my father's words, I know he's right. I don't want to admit it, but revenge isn't rushed.

I'm hot-headed. I act quickly, without question or reason.

Valentino sighs in the shadows, and I ask a question that's been plaguing me since I saw the contract, "Why would Cavallone even have agreed to me marrying her? I doubt he signed the contract that gives me control over his precious little princess."

Valentino's smile is dark, dangerous, his eyes glint with promise that his plan is filled with vengeance. "Because he didn't know she was marrying a De Rossi until his name was signed. I was there the day your father instigated it. Mattea was under the impression it was one of the Moretti sons. But… that was not the case." In our world, once you sign your name, it's done in blood. And there is no going back.

Narrowing my gaze, I ask, "But it still doesn't explain why Dad wants her specifically. What made him think she would be a good fit for me?"

"He didn't. None of us know if an arrangement will work, but the revenge he had planned was to end the Cavallone line once and for all," he informs me, which has my ears pricking with interest. "And this is the way to do it. She will take the De Rossi name, and once that happens, we kill the rest."

"I trust my father," I tell him. "I'll do it."

As the final curtain draws to a close, I know I

must leave. Rising from my seat, I pull out my cell phone and find a message from Mario informing me it's been done.

I've waited for too long to exact my revenge.

And it's time my little dancer knows that.

LUNA

I DON'T KNOW WHY I'M HERE.

Here being a place I've only heard whispers about.

Growing up within this life has allowed me to garner secrets that I probably shouldn't be privy to, but my father was always open and honest about who he was in this city—a man to be feared, and a man you could never cross because you'd end up dead.

At seventeen, I'm far too used to the life of Made men and violence.

"Why are we here?" I whisper to my uncle, Tommaso, as we walk up to Club Desperation, with a man named Mario following close behind. He's tall, far taller than Tommaso, and he's double my uncle's size.

Fear grips my chest as Tommaso holds my hand and gives it a small squeeze of reassurance, which doesn't calm my erratic heartbeat. "It's for your own good, *piccolo*," he mumbles, but doesn't look at me, causing anxiety to twist in my stomach.

The same butterflies I usually get before going up on stage now take flight in my stomach as we walk through the doors to find an opulent staircase that steals my breath. It's the first time I've ever been inside the club. My father may have been open about his life, but he never allowed me to come to a place like this.

And now I see why—it's breathtaking.

Not because of the dangerous men in suits, or the pretty women who are clearly submissive to them in the way they carry themselves, but because I've never seen something so exquisite before. I can't help but drink in every inch of the gothic architecture as we make our way to a table which we settle at without speaking.

From where we're sitting, the garden is visible, lit up by soft yellow bulbs that lead deep into the darkest shadows. A shiver wracks itself through me as I wonder just what lies in the woods that look like they could swallow me up.

The man, Mario, settles in opposite us, his dark gaze locked on my uncle. Anger juts his jaw, and a tick appears as he attempts to appear calm. But I can read people, and this man hates my uncle. He is handsome for an older man. I'm guessing he's probably in his early thirties. With a dark head of hair, and a gentle dusting of stubble, he looks like a male model walking off the pages of a magazine.

His suit is tailored perfectly for his broad shoulders, and the shirt attempts to hide his muscular chest, but does nothing of the sort. Instead, it only accentuates his formidable frame even more. His eyes are a shimmering gray, with long black lashes that sweep along his cheekbones with every blink.

Shifting in my seat, I swallow the lump of nerves in my throat. I can't find him attractive, he's a bad person. At least, that's what it seems like, because my uncle is a good man. He took over the family business after my father passed away.

Tearing my gaze away from Mario, I glance at Tommaso. He sits beside me, his fingers tangling around a pen that was lying on the long, wooden table. I haven't even changed my outfit after the show.

Drinks are set on the table in front of Mario and Tommaso, tumblers shimmering with a deep auburn liquid. The scent is strong, and I recognize it as whiskey. Father enjoyed his evening whiskey and a cigar. I always teased him and told him he reminded me of Don Corleone when he sat in his enormous wingback chair smoking and drinking. But since he was killed, there haven't been long nights in his office, reading his books, and asking him questions. He no longer offers me advice. There are no longer orders about where not to go, or who not to hang around with.

My father may have been the leader of a mafia family, but he was always just Dad to me. Someone who loved me dearly.

Since my mother died during childbirth, I was his *principessa*, his little girl. And nothing changed that.

"Where is he?" My uncle questions Mario as he fidgets with the pen. I'm not sure what is happening, but if Tommaso's demeanor is anything to go by, I have a feeling something bad is about to happen.

I feel a presence before I see him.

A tall, dark, handsome man with broad shoulders steps into view. It may be cliché, but that's exactly what he is. Mario rises to greet him, and so does my uncle. I don't move. Instead, I pin him with a glare because I have a feeling he's not here as a friend to our family.

I take him in as he greets Tommaso. His angular jaw is dusted with dark stubble, his eyes are the color of raven wings. His lips, full and pink, move slowly as he speaks in a low rumble. The baritone vibrating right through me.

His posture screams confidence and danger. The crisp white shirt he's wearing is unbuttoned just enough to tease the smooth olive skin beneath. I don't doubt that he is important, a man in charge. A leader.

When he settles into the chair opposite me, he finally pins me with a stare so fierce, my heart leaps into my throat, choking me. He doesn't speak, he merely watches me, as if he's assessing me, reading my nervous energy, and drinking it in like a vampire devouring the life force of a human.

It's Tommaso who speaks, "Luna, this is Mr. De Rossi." At the mention of his name, my blood turns to ice, and I freeze. Mr. De Rossi notices the corner of his mouth tips ever so slightly. It's the only movement, but it's clear he enjoys my discomfort.

I know who he is now.

The family who killed my father, and in retaliation, they killed his father. An eye for an eye. This is the life, I understand that, and I know he does too.

"Luna," my uncle nudges me, but I don't greet our guest. Instead, I lean back in the chair and stay silent. His mouth quirks again, and I can't deny he's breathtakingly handsome, but I hate him. And I make it known with a glare so fierce, I hope it burns him alive.

"Leave the girl, Tommaso, she's only here

because she needs to learn about her future," De Rossi says, his sneer making his handsome face even more threatening as he takes me in with those cold, dark eyes. It's as if night has taken up residence in his heart, and he no longer feels anything.

Dead inside.

"Let's get to it, shall we." He pulls out a thick envelope from his jacket pocket and sets it on the table before my uncle. I can feel eyes on us. I want to turn around, to see who's watching, but I don't. I'm not sure if De Rossi has bodyguards in the club, but my intuition tells me they're close by.

The opulence of the club belies what truly goes on inside. Tommaso opens the envelope, and I drag my attention back to the table to see him pull out a contract. On the top of the first page are the words *Contratto in Morte*.

My heart thuds against my ribs. My palms are sweaty as I rub them on my thighs. I glance at a few words. My name is clear on the white page, but it's the words beside it that make my breath catch.

…*Luna Isabella Cavallone, to be wed after her eighteenth birthday.*

"What is this?" I finally speak, and Enzo's brow arches in question. A man of slight movements that could probably make weak men cower. But I'm not a man, and I'm certainly not weak.

"This, my dear, is your future," Tommaso tells

me as he turns to look over at me. His hand poised, the pen ready to sign on a dotted line that will seal my fate. Only, it's not what I want.

"Why are you doing this? I can't marry him!"

"Lower your voice," the order comes from Enzo, his tone holding a silent threat that sends ice through my veins. "Your father understood he would lose everything when he came after my family, and when we paid him back for his violence, your family murdered my parents."

"Is this true?" I turn to my uncle, who sits quietly, making me think he's heard it all before. "Is this true, *zio*?" My voice cracks on the Italian word for uncle. My pleading tone doesn't even make him flinch with guilt. My father wasn't a good man, not by any means, but for him to do something like this to me. I'm not the enemy, and I'm certainly not one of the members of the family that wasn't loyal to him. To our name.

"Mattea left me in charge," Tommaso tells me as he scrawls his name on the page. "And I am only doing what is best for you."

"Best for me?" My voice raises a few octaves, causing the other men in the club to turn toward our table, interested in seeing what's happening. "This isn't best for me!"

"Tommaso," Enzo murmurs, his voice rigid with warning. "You get the girl under control, or I will be forced to do it myself."

I push the chair back and race from the room. The men who I had been convinced were watching us don't move toward me as I reach the exit. All the luxury that has been poured into the venue doesn't change it for what it is. This club is nothing more than a criminal's playground.

Outside, I make my way to Tommaso's car and lean my back against it. Inhaling deep breaths, I focus on calming my erratic heartbeat. I'm certain they'll come after me. He'll probably have me kidnapped and taken to his home, locked up in a room like some long-lost forgotten princess.

But if that monster thinks he's going to marry me, he has another thing coming. I'm not going to bow down to him, even if he is a Boss. My father would roll in his grave if he knew what I just did. It didn't matter what I wanted. Once an agreement or contract is signed, there is no backing out.

The only way to get out of this life is to die.

Would he kill me?

I don't know how much time passes, but when my uncle finds me, I'm slumped on the ground, my head on my knees and my arms wrapped around my legs. I'm shaking as the cold has now slowly sunk deep into the marrow of my bones, and I doubt I'll ever be able to get it out.

Tears have long since dried on my face, and

when I glance up, I see guilt written all over my uncle's face. "Why did you do that?"

He shrugs, buttoning his suit jacket as he reaches for the car key in his pocket. "It wasn't my decision, Luna."

My brows furrow. "Of course it is, you're my guardian," I insist, but he's already shaking his head before I can finish my sentence. Tommaso holds out a strong but wrinkled hand to me. I accept, but release it the moment I'm on my feet. "What's happening? Why do I have to marry Enzo de Rossi?" My questions hang in the air between us, a reminder that my father is no longer here. If he were, I would be privy to what had been agreed and why. But then again, I ran out of the club before I could learn the truth.

"This is your father's doing, Luna," Tommaso tells me earnestly. He locks his gray eyes on mine, and I find no lies in those metallic depths. It's then that I realize my life is over. "The contract was drawn up before your father died, instructing me to sign it in the event anything happened to him."

"And that was Father's last wish?" I sneer, causing Tommaso to flinch. As angry as I am, I can't feel sad about him losing his brother, because I lost my father. We both came out of this war as casualties. "I'm going to be a De Rossi," I tell him. "You realize the Cavallone line will die with me."

And as the words fall from my lips, I realize that was the plan all along. Revenge is a bittersweet game. It's not something done in haste. The slow, steady path always wins. And Salvatore De Rossi defeated my father one final time.

They may both be dead, but it's our family name that will forever be lost. My uncle will never marry, and he's never had children. I learned from eavesdropping as a child that Tommaso had problems with conceiving. He had a long-time partner, and they had both been into hospitals more times than I could count. But she left when she realized she would never have children.

Instead of becoming a good man, walking a straight path, Tommaso allowed his heartache to change him. He turned into a villain, and now, he's just signed away my life to our family's enemy.

"On your eighteenth birthday, you will go to him." There is finality in his words. I can't argue. I could try to run, but even then, I'll be found and murdered.

There is no escape.

Only a long life of servitude to one of the mafia's most notorious Bosses.

ENZO

I'VE WAITED PATIENTLY.

I'm no longer patient.

As I weave through evening traffic, my mind is on what is about to happen. She knows she's about to be given to me, but that's how this shit goes down. An arranged marriage between the heir and heiress of two powerful families is a business transaction, nothing more.

I learned all there was to know about her. Even before she realized who I was. Now, I'm going to collect what is owed to me. Even the night of signing the contract, I took her in, watching her from up close. She's not a woman to obey. This will not be easy. But I'll make my father proud, one way or another.

28

Luna Cavallone was livid. Rightly so, but there was nothing she could do about it. Of course, her uncle, Tommaso, tried to renege on the contract after she ran off, but with the threat of me having their soldiers and their two highest-ranking capos killed, ensured he signed on the dotted line.

A smile turns my lips up at the corners as I take in the setting sun. It's August, and as we head into fall, I look forward to the next few months as we plan the wedding.

The sky is shimmering with purples and pinks, soft colors, gentle sweeping hues of promises of another day ending. I know as I head to The Ruin, we're possibly walking into another war zone. If they don't try something tonight, I'll be surprised.

Butcher and Son, an old slaughterhouse that's been abandoned for as long as I've been alive, and sits like a beacon to criminal organizations within the New York area. It's where we can safely meet, whether it's for a deal with suppliers, or another Familia. It's the place that allows us to talk without the threat of being overheard. How poignant that the pretty young thing will give her life over to me in an old slaughterhouse.

A lamb to the slaughter.

Another smile graces my lips, but it's nothing short of sadistic. Happiness only comes through bloodshed. There is nothing else that brings me euphoria. I maim, I kill, and I fuck. But out of those three, fucking is merely basic instinct. The other two calm my inner devil.

Pulling up beside the familiar dark blue Mercedes Benz S Class of Valentino's, I kill the engine of my bike, before swinging my leg over the bike. I crunch the gravel with my boots and take in my men, who followed behind me in the SUV. I prefer being on the motorcycle. I love the freedom it offers, even though it's dangerous in my line of work, and with my last name, but I'd rather feel the cool wind on my face than be cooped up in the backseat of one of my many cars.

There are already a few SUVs parked in the lot, blacked-out windows for privacy while traveling. And I'm guessing those are bulletproof as well. It's needed in our line of work.

I leave the helmet on my seat before I zip up my leather jacket. A chuckle escapes my lips because I know my father will be insulted by the fact that I'm not wearing a suit. There are outfits for different occasions, and this one didn't need me to be dressed in black tie.

I make my way to the derelict warehouse. The roof doesn't offer any protection from the elements any longer, but the weather has held for the meeting tonight, so it's not needed. The doors are guarded by De Rossi men and they offer me a nod when I saunter by.

Inside, Valentino is talking to a handful of our soldiers who have no doubt been brought here to keep us safe. These men will die for me, and for their capos. The loyalty that lies within a Familia is strong, second to none.

"You're late," Valentino says, his tone icy, as I reach him. His dark eyes lock on me, taking me in from head to toe, and I can feel his annoyance at my apparel.

Shrugging it off, I offer him a smile. "I had things to do before I meet my wife." The chill in the air drops to below zero when Valentino's stormy expression pins itself on me. "I'm serious."

"Don't fuck this up, it's what your father wanted," he murmurs as footsteps sound from the door. *But it's not what I wanted.* But I don't bother arguing with him. "It's the only revenge we will get," he tells me. "And make sure to leave with her as soon as possible. I don't need her knowing anything more than what she should. Once you're gone, we will handle Tommaso."

I can't say anything in response. I can't ask what his plan is, because the Cavallones have arrived, causing Valentino to straighten as if he wasn't just perturbed at my tardiness and lack of suit. He's nothing if not composed around others, especially when it comes to our enemies. Just like my father was. I don't look at them for a long while as they come to a stop in front of us.

"De Rossi," the deep baritone of Tommaso echoes, and I offer a silent nod. "You've taken many of my men, and you've made sure I can't do anything about it. My brother would be heartbroken to see his clan in such disrepair." The anger in his voice is pure fire as he delivers his words.

That's when I meet his gaze and smile. "When you start a war, you should be prepared to finish it," I tell him, keeping my tone cool, aloof, as if I'm not at all concerned about the lives we've taken. And I'm not. I learned from my father, and I will never feel guilt for this life. Salvatore De Rossi never concerned himself with acts of the past. It's the future that always had his focus.

"Let it be known that I will get my niece back," Tommaso hisses through clenched teeth with a jaw ticking, vehemence cutting into his voice, into his words.

The corner of my mouth tips upward, a satisfied smirk circling my lips as I take a step forward. "Who knows, perhaps I'll return her after I'm done with her." My promise is filled with danger as I take another few steps toward the man who won't live to see another day. Only, he doesn't know it yet. He's much shorter than I am, and when I stop inches from him, I tower over the older man. "But when

I do, she won't be in the same pristine condition you delivered her in. Now, tell me, Tommaso," I murmur, ensuring he cowers from my tone. "Where is my little wife?"

Anger vibrates through him, his hands fist at his sides and his jaw ticks with barely restrained violence, but he won't lash out. He knows that if he tries something, he'll be dead before he can blink.

We've surrounded them. Our men are ready, waiting for something to go wrong. My hand is trained on my knife that's comfortably sheathed at the small of my back. I don't go anywhere without it. And meeting one of my enemies is more than reason enough to ensure I can slice into his wrinkled, tanned flesh before he can spew his venom.

"Bring her in," he orders, and I take a step back, but I don't look away from the old man. Every small nuance he emits, I take in. He's afraid. I've become accustomed to reading people, and he's not at all difficult to read.

Too bad the men will kill him before he walks out of here tonight. I wish I could be here to watch, but like Valentino said, I need to keep Luna away from the violence for as long as possible. It will make it easier on her when she learns she's alone in this world with only me to lean on.

I briefly wish it was her father before me. He died thinking his daughter will sleep beside a

Moretti, but instead, she has me. I wish he knew her last name will be De Rossi, it would have grated at him because if he knew I'll be the one fucking her, making her cry and scream would have most definitely made his blood boil. Even so, a smile cuts across my face.

Tommaso notices the flare of rage in his eyes sparks like a wildfire taking out a forest in its path. But there is no other violence from him. This is one of those moments where the saying, *if looks could kill,* comes to mind.

"*Zio?*" Her voice is like a lyrical melody, stealing my attention from her uncle, but for a long moment, I don't glance her way. Instead, I inhale deeply, basking in the gentle fragrance that hits my senses as she nears us—candied apples.

A memory slams into my chest, into my mind as I recall my mother making them at Christmas. I was only ten at the time and she would make sure I got the biggest one. I would help her in the kitchen, twirling the sticky confection until I was drenched in it. My mouth and hands a deep red, but as I grew up, got older, the claret that now stains me is far from the innocence of sugary treats.

I finally twist my body to face her. To look at the woman who will soon be my wife, and to say I wasn't ready for it, would be an understatement. She's dressed in a pair of black tights that hug her long shapely legs. Her feet are hidden in a pair of soft pink ballet flats.

Her hair is bound in a bun at the back of her head, and her delicate neck is smooth and creamy. She's not as tanned as the girls I remember from southern Italy. She's fair, like a porcelain doll. Her back is straight, her shoulders back as if she's not afraid. *She should be.*

She stops beside her uncle. Even though she's tall, her head barely reaches his. And if she were beside me, she'd be at least a head and a bit shorter than my towering frame. Her hips have a slight curve, giving her an hourglass figure.

Her chest is barely there, her tits more than a handful. The top she's wearing is pastel pink, just like her shoes, and it's tight, showing off her slender frame. Her spine straight, chin tipped back with confidence, even amongst violent men. All that elegance and poise comes from her ballet classes.

My cock throbs at the sight of her sweet, candy innocence. And I want nothing more than to tarnish the pristine pink of her clothes and the porcelain smoothness of her skin. I swallow back the lump in my throat and focus on the here and now.

She's exquisite.

More than I imagined.

But then, I have been stalking her like a creep in the shadows.

"Luna," Tommaso mumbles as he turns to the girl who's just entered, flanked by two bulky men in suits. "I need you to go now," he informs her. "I told you there is no other way this plays out."

"But—"

He shakes his head, pinning her with a glare so fierce, it has her cowering, and it's the first time I see true fear in her expression. And I would be lying if I said it didn't make my dick hard. The little dancer is capable of being scared, which will make this even more fun.

For a long time, she just stares at her uncle before she silently nods. Then, she turns those eyes on me, the soft olive green that greets me holds anger as she looks me over. I don't move, allowing her to take me in from head to toe before she flicks those orbs on mine.

"Is this the only way you can get a woman?" she sneers, stepping up to me, her shoulders back and her chin tipped in defiance. My desire only seems to warm for her, heating my blood, as she stops in front of me. "It's a shame." The little dancer skates her gaze over me once more, her lip curling in disgust, and I can't stop the chuckle that vibrates through my chest.

"Fire." I tip my head to the side, regarding her with cool admiration. "I like it. More than I enjoyed you running from the table where I was seated."

Before she can respond, I tip my chin toward my men, who grab her arms and drag her from the warehouse. Her screams bounce off the walls as she curses me to hell.

Don't worry, sweetheart, I'm there already.

"Nice doing business with you," I tell Tommaso, before I offer Valentino a look and nod in agreement to kill the bastard. Turning on my heel, I head out, following behind the two men I have that are trying to get my new wife into the back of the waiting town car.

I really should go with her and try to get to know her, but since I have my bike, I don't bother offering her any more attention before sliding my leg over the cool metal and shrugging on the helmet. The rumble of the engine growls between my legs and I take off, knowing my men won't be far behind as they escort my bride to the penthouse.

And when I get there, I'm going to make sure she knows exactly who owns her now.

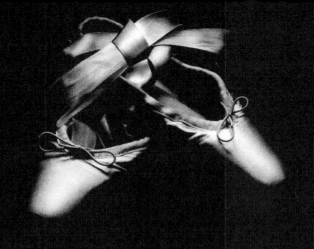

LUNA

Anger is the only thing I feel when I walk into the immaculate living room. His home is nothing more than my prison. It's furnished in darkness and draped in violence. Everything that just happened confirms what I already knew. The prince of the De Rossi Familia is my future husband, and there's nothing I can do about it. The contract stands. My uncle finalized it and now I find myself in the devil's lair.

The night the paperwork was signed, I was furious, but over the past few weeks, I've allowed that emotion to stew, and now I'm drowning in rage.

"This is where you'll wait for the boss," one of the men who brought me here says in a rough voice. He's tall and scary. His shoulders span the width of the doorway, and his hands are clasped in front of his stomach. He looks every bit as violent as Enzo. "Don't try anything because we are right outside, and if we have to run after you, you might get hurt," he informs me with a smirk that tells me I *will* get hurt. "And that will only upset the boss." He gestures with his head, his eyes pinned on me as if he doesn't trust me. I wouldn't trust me either because I need to get out of here, but being in the penthouse doesn't leave room for escape.

"And how many women have you locked in his apartment before?" I sneer, but he doesn't answer. He merely shakes his head and chuckles before shutting the door in my face.

I turn to take in the living area. Even if I wanted to run, there's nowhere to go. And I don't think the man I'm here to marry will take too kindly to my antics. Not that I care if he hates me or not, because I most definitely hate him, but I don't know if he'll hurt my uncle if I were to disobey him.

Time and again, I told my papa that he should walk away from ruling the empire his former capo left to him, but he refused. Yes, we were a force to be reckoned with a long time ago, but over the years, my father trusted the wrong men. And it brought us to a point of desperation. When I learned the Boss of the De Rossi clan, as well as his wife were killed, I knew my life was over. I didn't fight the contract. I didn't even ask Tommaso to request another form of payment. This is the life I'd been born into and it's the life I've come to accept. Since I was a little girl, I realized I would never marry for love.

In this life, there are no choices.

Not for me, anyway.

I'm here because my father fucked up.

I'm no stranger to blood. Not even death scares me, but knowing my papa is a killer, that does something to a girl. I grew up around men who have blood staining their hands, knowing about the mafia, learning about princes and princesses who ruled every criminal organization known to man.

And I learned my fair share about my future husband.

Enzo de Rossi wasn't just any Underboss; he was *the* Underboss.

And when my family had his parents murdered, he stepped up. He took over the reins of the De Rossi Familia, and he became the king. He was a man that was whispered about, older than me by a good fifteen years. At thirty-three, he's one of the youngest bosses, and is rumored to be the cruelest.

I first heard his name when I started my senior year in high school. All the girls there talked about was who they'd be married off to. They were excited. I wasn't. All my friends knew of Enzo de Rossi. He was Underboss at the time, and the fixer of the family. He would kill those who wronged the De Rossi name, and he did so without mercy.

All my friends crushed on him.

They *wanted* to be his wife.

And yet, here I am, hating the fact that I will soon say the words *I do* to a man I hate, but begrudgingly also respect. He has done some deplorable things in his life, but he seems to have done them because he needed to. The vile people he killed suggested he did not do it for fun.

According to my father, he enjoyed his position within the Familia. He loved the jobs his own father would send him on. I've eavesdropped far too many times on conversations a girl like me had no right hearing. Enzo is a legend within the clans. He is meticulous in his torture, and merciless in his kills.

But if I compare Enzo to the men who worked for my father, I realize Enzo isn't evil, despite my belief that he's a monster. Each kill he's made, every person whose life he's taken, had all wronged his family. He never afforded them mercy, which means he may not show me any either.

He will see me as one of them, and no matter what my last name will be, I will never truly be a De Rossi.

Which is why I know I need an upper hand, or something of the sort, to make sure he doesn't kill me on the first night. I did my fair share of research on Enzo since the night of the contract signing.

And that's when I learned two things about my future husband.

Men age like a fine wine.

And Enzo de Rossi is an exquisite vintage.

Sighing, I move through the apartment. Since I'm alone, I don't bother fighting, knowing there are two vicious bodyguards are right outside. One thing I learned from my father was that I should choose my battles. I may want to stab Enzo in the jugular for making me marry him, but, I know that if I choose my battles with him with a clear mind, I may get through this.

I take in his apartment. An intimate dining room sits to the left of the entrance, and to the left of it is the kitchen, which I don't pay much attention to. The windows in the open plan living room are floor to ceiling, with an arch close to the top, which gifts it an appearance of a chapel of sorts. The views of New York greet me, the lights twinkling as I pass by the fireplace and head down the hall.

There are four doors. Pushing one open, I find a luxurious bathroom with spa bath and large shower. The next room is a bedroom with a single bed and a few bits of furniture. When I move deeper down the hallway, I open the next door to my right and find a beautiful bedroom decked out in soft blue furnishings, an enormous king-sized bed, along with a chaise longue which overlooks the city.

There are no photos with family memories, nothing that would confirm anyone *actually* lives here. Enzo's house is as much a mystery as he is. The man is a ghost, apart from the photos captured of him attending expensive dinners and gala events with beautiful women on his arm. I noticed that none of these women were featured a second or third time with him. He's well-known in this town for enjoying meaningless, no-string attachments. Nothing more.

That shouldn't bother me as much as it does, but I can't stop the jealousy from coursing through my veins. It's stupid to be bitter over someone I don't love, or even care for, but deep down, knowing he'll soon be my husband does stupid shit to me. Shit, I didn't expect or care for. I don't like being vulnerable. I can defend myself, if need be, but right now, I feel like a fish out of water.

Turning my attention back to my surroundings, I focus on exploring more of my new home before Enzo returns. I find a walk-in closet in what I assume will be my bedroom. It's filled with designer dresses and outfits in mostly red, white, black, and one stunning gold one. There are a few blouses in a variety of shades, but it seems my fiancé likes a specific color palette of evening dresses. I leave the closet and wander deeper into the room to find a marble tiled bathroom boasting a spa bath. This one larger than the other and includes a shower which I'm almost certain can fit at least four people comfortably.

Everything is pristine, from the silver taps to the exquisitely tiled floors. Each bedroom I venture into, three including mine, are all carpeted in lush fabric. But my interest is piqued when I move to the last door in the apartment. Pushing it open, I step inside a room that screams masculine energy. It's dark, foreboding, and an icy shiver zips down my spine. This is without a doubt, Enzo's bedroom.

Everything is black—from his bedsheets to his pillows, even the lampshades are raven-colored. The dark walls seem to close in on the enormous space, but it makes it *feel* warmer. I run my fingertips over the material of the comforter, the softness of the silk under my touch tingles on my fingertips. I wonder briefly if I'll leave my scent on them, and for a long moment, I worry about invading his space.

But I convince myself that I'm going to be his wife soon, and everything he owns will be mine. With that thought in my mind, I move silently through his personal space. The carpet is a charcoal gray, the curtains match, offering a cloak of darkness the other rooms didn't possess.

Fear grips me when I notice a cabinet in the corner of the room. Glass doors display leather belts, a whip, and three shimmering steel blades.

I've heard stories about him.

I've listened to the whispers of violence that he's exacted on people he hates, and yet, I find myself enthralled by the stranger who I'm about to marry. All those whispers overheard from the men in my father's clan, every violent act and merciless killing, replay in my mind as I recall them.

My future husband is a murderer.

A forewarning that I shouldn't be in here, but I can't stop my curiosity from piquing when I reach his closet. Inside, I find nothing but black and white. The crisp, stark cotton shirts against inky suits and torn jeans show just how much this man revels in the darkness.

I head to his bathroom, finding the same color-scheme bleeding through from the bedroom. Black marble tiles, with white veins tinged with gold. There is no longer a doubt in my mind that the bedroom I visited earlier will be mine, and this one will always be his private domain.

Even as his wife, I doubt that I'll ever be allowed in here again. For a brief moment, a split second, sadness overwhelms me, and I realize that no matter what I do, I'll never be someone he loves.

I'm nothing more than a contract.

A twisted obsession for him to use to fulfill his ultimate goal—revenge for my father's actions.

ENZO

When I reach the top floor of my apartment building, I find Mario and Adriano flanking the door. Both dressed in black, they offer me a nod as I near them.

"All quiet?" I ask, gesturing toward the entrance of my home.

Mario nods. "She's been warned that we'll be right outside. I haven't heard her breaking anything, but then again, she's a fiery one. She may be waiting for you on the other side with a knife or something," he tells me, a small smile glinting on his lips.

"I am not averse to tying her to the fucking bedframe," I inform him. "I need you both at the door while I'm out tomorrow. Valentino wants to meet with the Morettis. Franco is back from Italy, and I have a feeling we may garner support against the Irish mob that's moving into town. I can't take her with me, she's too volatile now."

"Understood," Mario says with a nod of his head. "If you need me beside you, I'll be there. We can get Thiago here. He arrived from London a couple of days ago."

"I didn't realize he's back. Yes, call him in and you can join me in the meeting." I nod, knowing that Thiago is one of the best. He usually looks after the outfit in London, but if he's in the city, I'd rather have him here than someone else. Adriano is good, but I would feel better having two men watching Luna. Because as much as I know she can't escape, I don't trust her.

Not yet.

Perhaps never.

"You'll stay here with Thiago until I return tomorrow night," I inform Adriano quickly before I grab the door handle and twist it.

"Understood, sir," he responds. He's new to the clan, being brought here from Black Hollow Isle. A place where our Familia has trained the soldiers who work for us. A school where students learn how to kill, while getting a higher education. Since he's arrived, Adriano has proven himself loyal when he took a bullet for me a couple of months ago when we went to war with the Cavallones. Now, I trust him with my life.

I take my leave of the men and push open the front door, only to be met with silence. Without calling to her, I make my way into the empty living room. For a moment, I wonder if she found a way to escape without my guards noticing her. But that won't be possible since everything is locked up tight. Even the fire escape only opens with my fingerprint, so if she has fled, she would've jumped off the balcony. I doubt she'd risk her life that way.

Shrugging off my jacket, I hang it on the coat hook and head deeper into the apartment. When I pass by each of the open doors, I realize she's clearly been exploring her new home.

By the time I reach my bedroom, I'm tense. I don't allow anybody in this space. It's mine and mine alone. But as I step into my bedroom, I hear the distinct sound of the metal hangers in my closet being pushed back and forth. It's then that I know I've found my little dancer.

The perfect princess of the Cavallone clan is standing in my walk-in closet, touching my clothes. Two emotions course through me at seeing her fingertips against the material of my shirts—desire and hatred.

There is a fine line between love and hate, but this twisted need inside me makes me want to see her cry for invading my sanctuary. For handling my things. Those aren't for her to touch, at least not yet.

Once she takes my name, she'll be a slave to my needs. Perhaps I'll make her my own personal maid. She can clean and cook while I'm working. I'm by no means old school, believing that women should be in the kitchen, pregnant, but with her, I can't stop the heat from flooding my veins when I imagine her perfect body swollen with my son.

Beauty is in the eye of the beholder.

And *she* is most certainly exquisite.

I shake that thought from my mind as I watch her touching my clothes before she drops her hand and grips the metal bar that holds my suit pants. They're about waist high to her, and she shifts them around to make space for her delicate hands.

It's then that the ballet training she's been accustomed to shines through when she does some silly little pose, which pushes her tight ass out and curves her back beautifully. I could fuck her into submission just like that.

I fold my arms across my chest and lean against the bedframe. The four-poster bed will be a place she'll come to know well, but she'll never sleep beside me. As hard as her beauty makes my cock, she's still the enemy.

I watch her lift one arm into the air, curving it back until she's staring at the ceiling, her other hand lightly holding onto the metal to keep her balance as she raises up on her tip toes. The movement has her calves appearing even more prominent, the cutting lines of her muscled, yet lean legs have me throbbing against my zipper.

Fuck, how I'd love to bend her in all the positions I can while she takes me deep inside that hourglass figure. I clear my throat, tired of watching and needing to have the space to myself and free from desire for the woman I hate. The sound jolts her. She snaps her gaze to mine as a soft gasp tumbles free from her plump, soft pink lips.

"I-I…" she mumbles, racing from the closet and shutting the door before she stops in front of me. The shock slowly wears off, but the guilt that she'd been caught in here is etched on her pretty face. She's got an elfin look about her. Raven-hued hair, soft pale skin with a beautifully curled mouth. Her eyes are the softest shade of green, while her brows are dark as they frame the almond-shaped orbs.

She has high cheekbones which are pinkened from embarrassment. I want to taunt her some more, just to see how dark that shade will go, but I'm not in the mood to have her in my space, not yet anyway.

"I'll show you to your bedroom," I tell her without acknowledging the fact that I caught her snooping. Turning on my heel, I head for the door before she speaks again.

"I need to know what you're going to do with

me," she says, her voice strong and confident compared to moments ago. It's the same poise she displayed in the warehouse, and I decide I like it, even though I know it will get her into trouble with me.

I don't bother responding as I head into the hallway with her padding behind me. Her steps are quick, soft, and almost silent. But I hear her. I *feel* her. I stop outside the guest bedroom I had made up for her when I realized there was no going back on this arrangement. It was the best course of action. The room has been waiting for her for years, and I hope she likes it. Shaking my head at the errand thought, I fist my hands in frustration at the idea of me wanting her to be comfortable.

She's here to pay for her father's sins, not to be coddled like a princess. She may have come from a home where everyone treated her like royalty, but she's no queen in the De Rossi clan.

Not yet.

Not until I allow her to be.

"This will be your bedroom," I tell her, ignoring her earlier question. "You'll stay in here until I call for you. In the morning, I'll have my men outside the door. If you need anything, ask them and they'll get it for you."

"Enzo—"

I spin on my heel when she whispers my name.

Anger surges through me that this girl can affect me in ways no woman ever has. My hand shoots out as my fingers grip her neck in a tight hold. A dick-hardening gasp tumbles from her mouth, and I want nothing more than to swallow every sound she makes.

"You'll refer to me as Mr. De Rossi until I say otherwise," I say, my tone filled with unadulterated venom. "Only my friends and family call me Enzo. You're neither of those." *Not yet anyway,* my mind adds silently. "Nod if you understand," I instruct my sweet little dancer.

She obeys and I release her, moving away to inhale a breath that doesn't fill my senses with *her.* In the bedroom, I turn, glancing over my shoulder to wait for her to follow. When she does, I look away, needing to focus on anything else but the way she heats my blood.

"You know, I'm not just some toy you can push around," Luna tells me as she sidles by me as if I didn't just have my fingers wrapped around her neck. She heads for the window, which overlooks the city below. The lights are twinkling, the Big Apple alive with possibility, and in the distance, the sky has turned an inky shade which matches her hair.

For the first time in my life, I'm speechless. I've never had a woman in my apartment for longer than it took for her to make me come. And then, she would be out on her ass before she can thank me for the pleasure.

This woman will be my wife soon.

"You're here to repay the De Rossi Familia for your father's sins," I inform her, but I'm sure she already knows that. I watch her for a long while and when she finally sighs, nodding in response.

She turns to regard me then. "My father may have made bad choices in his life, but with your parents—"

My hand is on my knife in seconds, and I'm closing the distance between me and my new bride before she can finish her sentence. Her fear is palpable when I shove her back against the window. Her back flat against the cool glass as my arm rests on her windpipe. The sleek, silver blade whispers a threat against her cheek. "If you ever speak of what happened again, if you ever try to say your father was in the right to do what he did, or if you ever, ever mention my parents again," I hiss, my words dripping poison onto the space between us. "I will end you just like they sliced my parents into ribbons. Mattea Cavallone may not have their blood on his hands, but the Cavallones are stained nonetheless."

She tips her head back, her chin lifting in defiance at me. "Do it," she says, pushing against the blade that's kept me safe each time I've wielded it against an enemy. The smooth skin of her delicate neck darkens slightly from the scrape of metal, and my cock throbs against my zipper.

Pushing away from her before she hurts herself, I narrow my gaze, locking my stare on hers. "Don't tempt me, little dancer." Tipping my head to the side, I can't stop the sinister smile from curling my lips. "Get some sleep. Tomorrow, we get to know each other." I turn and make my way to the exit. This time, I shut myself out of her bedroom before I lean against the smooth wooden surface, my eyes closed, my head tipped back against the door.

Pulling my cell phone from my pocket and I hit call on Mario's number before making my way to the living room where I pour a double shot of smoky Macallan. When he doesn't answer the first time, I try again, and that's when he picks up.

"Have you killed her already?" he asks in greeting, but the amusement in his tone tells me he thinks I'll probably murder the pretty little dancer before I say *I do*.

"No," I bite out before swallowing back the deep amber liquid. The burn trails its way down my throat, and I revel in the fire as it reaches my stomach. "I can't have her live here."

"She's going to be your wife, Enzo," he tells me in a tone that frustrates me. This is why I've been friends with him for as long as I have, he's levelheaded where I am more inclined to go with murder, before going along with this stupid idea my father had, that me marrying someone, will settle me down.

"She's invaded my bedroom, my closet, even my fucking head," I finally bite out. "She's a nuisance, and I don't like the distraction. I have work to do and I can't concentrate if she's going to go snooping around my house."

Mario sighs. I picture him rolling his eyes and smiling as he listens to my frustrations. "Get to know her, give her a chance."

"Are you saying I'll eventually love her?" I sneer, the thought causing my body to burn hot with anger. "She's a Cavallone, the only way I'll ever feel anything for her is when I finally get to slice all that pretty porcelain skin from her bones."

My best friend chuckles. The sound so foreign to me now. He used to laugh around my mother all the time. She would always bring out the best in him. And that's why I'll never love Luna. She's a reminder of what my family has become.

I think back to a conversation I had once with my father when he brought up arranged marriage. I didn't think he'd go through with it at the time.

"Listen to me," Dad says, his voice taking on a saddened tone. "I didn't love your mother when we first

got married, either. It takes time in situations like these."

I pour another drink before walking over to the balcony doors and staring out into the night. "You both always seemed so in love, so perfect?" I never thought of myself as a husband, that I would settle down and have one woman in my bed for the rest of my life. It wasn't in my plan. All I wanted was to take over the Familia from my father and ensure that nobody could ever overthrow us. We've built a strong foundation, one I know is solid, but if I had someone beside me, maybe it would be easier. The thought of a woman walking into my life, being forced to marry me, and become part of my family, I'm not sure know how long it will last.

"My father, your grandfather, arranged my marriage to your mother. The moment she walked into my life, I didn't think it would work because she was too stubborn."

I can't help but smile at that. My mother truly was a force to be reckoned with. And she was the only person who could bring my father to his knees. But that's not me. I'm not a man who will ever give into someone else.

"I'm not you," I tell him easily before swallowing back my whiskey and setting the glass down. Pushing open the balcony doors, I step out into the night, and close my eyes. "I never wanted a family. The clan. The violence. I don't want anyone else to be a part of it. I like being alone."

"Do you?" he challenges quickly, and I ponder his question. When I don't respond right away, he sighs. "*Perhaps you need to go out on a job, get all that frustration out and then when you get home, you can sit down and consider this as an option. Any woman who walks into our family will have responsibilities.*"

"*What? To marry me and give me heirs who I can train to become killers like I am?*" I know I'm taunting him, but he's right, I need to get out of this place and get the violence out of my blood before I even think about a wedding, a wife, and a forever.

"*It's not as bad as you're making it out to be. You're almost thirty now. Once that milestone comes, you're going to need to step into my shoes.*" The only time my father ever let his guard down is around me. It used to only be with my mom, but he's slowly been allowing me in. And I get to see the man my mother fell in love with.

"*I know. Those are big shoes to fill, but I am ready. I've been ready to take over the clan for years.*" He knows I'm right. When I started working for him when I was sixteen., I didn't think I could make it this far, but now, as Underboss, I'm next in line. And I'm ready. This life courses through my veins. I was born to lead.

"Her scent is all over my bedroom. I don't like it."

Mario laughs once more. "Good. I think it will challenge you. I know you'll enjoy taunting your new toy, just don't kill her yet, yeah?" His chuckle makes me smile.

"Yeah," I tell him before hanging up. I take in the city below me, the sprawling Big Apple, which seems to swallow you whole if you don't fight it. I was born and bred in this place, and yet, it's felt so distant recently. When I was younger, I reveled in the parties and the girls, now, I feel as if putting on my father's shoes and running the Familia to make him proud has added a burden on my shoulders I didn't expect. Which is why I need to go on a job. Most times, I delegate, but tomorrow is special. We've found two ex-clan members who went rogue, and I'm going to enjoy torturing information from them.

Sighing, I step back into the living room, only to find Luna in the kitchen. The open plan space allows me to see most of the living area from the balcony doors. As she leans up on her tiptoes, I drink in the soft curves and defined lines of her legs. A dancer's body.

My cock enjoys the view, but my brain reminds me who she is.

"What the fuck are you doing out of your room?" I should have locked the door. Made sure she can't leave. It's not like she'll piss herself since there is an en-suite, but it will allow me the space I need without needing to see her.

She lowers to her small feet before glancing at me from over her shoulder. "I'm looking for something to eat," she informs me before shutting the cabinet door. In her hand is a box of cereal, which I'm almost certain is past its sell by date. When she lifts the flap of the box, her nose creases in a way that makes her face seem even younger than her almost nineteen years.

"There's bread in the cupboard and some cheese in the fridge," I bite out, aggravation taking a hold of me as I make my way toward her. I don't eat at home. I don't cook. Perhaps my new wife will do all that for me and more.

As she reaches for the cabinet door, I don't miss how the tee she's wearing rides up her thighs. Her curves and those lithe legs taunt me from under the hem.

"Do you want something?" Luna questions, innocence flickering in her tone like a candle in a gentle breeze. She doesn't flinch when I pin her with a hard glare. She doesn't even cower when I close the distance between us. Her hold on the bread doesn't tighten like I expect it to.

"There is a lot I want. I'm just not sure you're up to giving it to me," I tell her, keeping my tone cool and aloof. My words cause a slight tremble on her lips, but the corners quirk before she shakes her head.

"I'm not afraid of you," she tells me adamantly.

I regard her through narrowed eyes before I ask,

"And why, pray tell, is that, little dancer?"

Her cheeks heat at the nickname I've afforded her, but she doesn't shrink under my towering form. If anything, she only seems to straighten her back and tip her head back with confidence. "Because I've spent my life around men like you," she informs me with no inflection in her voice. "And they all think they have bigger dicks than the next. Only, it seems those who wave it around have nothing worth looking at."

A chuckle vibrates in my chest and escapes my lips without me thinking about it. It's the first time in a long time someone has made me laugh, without constraint, and certainly without having to fake it.

Luna doesn't seem amused. She merely watches me for a while until I silence myself and lock my gaze with hers. She has beautiful eyes. It's the first time I've looked at her, properly looked at her, and I can't deny she's breathtaking.

"Trust me when I say this, little dancer, if I were to bring my cock anywhere near you, you'd run a mile. I can and will easily break you in half." There's no hint of a smile on my face, and there's no amusement in my tone.

Luna's mouth falls open into an O shape, which makes my body respond with a throb. "Then I suppose you should keep it away from me then," she retorts hotly before spinning on her heel and busying herself with her sandwich. But it doesn't hide the blush that shaded her cheeks when she truly realized what I said.

Shaking my head, I turn and head for the living room, which seems to be an escape for now. I need another drink, one that will hopefully calm me the fuck down. Every thought in my mind is about what I could do to my fiancée. A pretty, little dancer who could so easily break underneath me.

The thought of gripping her delicate throat, squeezing while my cock owns her, makes me throb once more. I can't stop the images of her crying as I thrust into her body from dancing through my thoughts, just like she twirls on stage, so the reel plays in a loop in my mind.

And I know this isn't going to be as easy as my father thinks.

LUNA

Pacing the carpet, I sigh in frustration as the sun rises on a new day. I haven't seen Enzo since last night, and once he left me in the bedroom, locked up like a prisoner, it was as if I were alone in the apartment.

Silence greeted me for hours before I fell asleep. And when I did, it wasn't peaceful. Dreams of his violence invaded my mind, leaving me tossing and turning until I gave up trying to get some rest. I'm not sure what his plans for me are, but Father must have told him about my schooling. I need to practice my dancing, even while cooped up like a captive.

What he did last night, when I taunted him in his personal space, should have scared me, but it didn't. Nothing he does can make me fear him because I've grown up in this world, and I've seen some things that will make even the strongest stomachs turn. And that's what my fiancé will come to realize.

When the lock clicks on my bedroom door, I turn to watch it open and a man, one I've come to recognize appears on the threshold. Mario Errani. He's dressed in a black, tailored suit which has clearly been cut just for his broad frame.

I cross my arms over my chest, wanting to keep myself from breaking down and asking him to release me from my servitude. It's stupid because I know there is no escape, but it can't hurt me trying. I can't show weakness in front of Enzo, but perhaps one of the men who works for him will see how wrong this all is. "What are you doing in here?"

"Good morning, Ms. Cavallone," he greets as he steps inside, taking in the room with his gray eyes. There's a dark flicker in his eyes when he looks at the bed, but seconds later, it's gone. He fiddles with his cuff links before he turns to me.

"What are you doing in here?" I ask again, frustration causing me to bristle. I note the small smile that tilts his lips before he moves deeper into my room. He doesn't answer me for a long time, but I don't move. I watch him from my perch near the window. If he were to attack, I could jump. I'd probably break something, but it may free me from this oaf of a man.

That's a lie.

He's no oaf.

He must be over six-feet tall, with broad shoulders and a jawline that could slice through marble. His tanned, olive skin compliments his dark hair. Silver eyes remind me of a predator and his full lips make his mouth intoxicating to watch as it shifts in tiny movements.

"My boss is a man who doesn't like to be questioned," Mario finally speaks, revealing he the familiar deep baritone I heard the night my uncle signed the contract. "He always gets what he wants. There is never any doubt when he speaks, people revel in his words and obey with no retort."

I meet his gaze, holding it, before tipping my chin back in a fake show of confidence which I most definitely don't feel. "Why are you telling me this?"

He takes in my stance, his eyes roving over me, from head to toe and back to my face, where he holds my stare hostage. As much as I want to look away, I find I can't. Strength and confidence oozes from him as he settles on the bed and finally gives me a big smile. One that makes his eyes sparkle like metal in sunlight.

"I need you to know that no matter what you do to him, say to him, he'll never let you leave this place. You're his now. And even though he doesn't love you, you will be his wife until you take your final breath."

The reminder of what I've been forced into sends chills down my spine. "Let me make something clear. I may be young, but this life…" I wave my hand to gesture around me. "Is what I've grown up in. I know about the violence, the darkness, and the bullshit that comes with my contract. Your *boss* may be next in line, but I'm a princess within my Familia. I've been born and bred to rule, and if he can't accept a queen by his side, then he should kill me now." I hold up my finger to silence him when he opens his mouth before I continue my tirade. "And let me make another thing clear. I never once asked him to love me. I may not have chosen him as my husband, and I'm not deluded to think he wants me as a wife, but we're both adults and can live with the lives our families have chosen for us."

Mario stares at me wide-eyed and slack jawed. His gaze lands on my hands and it's only then I realize I'm trembling with anger. My stomach twists at what I've just done—begging to be killed instead of marrying a man who will never love me.

A slow clap breaks the tension in the room and my stare that's been locked on the stranger for the last few minutes moves toward the sound. Enzo steps into the room, his suit pants are a dark blue and they hug every toned muscle of his legs. A crisp white shirt with the top three buttons undone looks like it's been molded to his toned frame, and the sleeves are rolled up to his elbows, gifting me a glimpse of tanned skin.

"What a sassy little thing you are," he says with a sadistic smirk, curling his lips. A glint catches my eye, and I notice his belt is also a holster, a blade in place of a gun in a leather sheath. The same knife he wielded last night.

"I was just telling it like it is." Once more, I cross my arms, holding myself steady because I suddenly feel dizzy. They're both double my size, and I know there is no way I'll be able to fight my way out of this. The only thing I have to bargain with is my body, and I don't intend giving that up.

Not to them.

Ever.

Enzo drops his gaze, his focus on the floor as he leans against the door frame, his arms folded, which only seems to cause corded veins to bulge from his forearms. Everything south of my belly button tightens, and I swallow back a moan of appreciation.

He's a killer.

A violent, obsessive monster.

"Perhaps you should keep those pretty lips shut, little dancer," he murmurs as he lifts his hand, scrubbing at the darkened jawline of his handsome, Adonis-like face. His beard shadows the angles, but it doesn't diminish just how handsome he truly is.

"You'd like that. Wouldn't you?" I challenge. "A submissive little pet for you to toy with." My words are biting, but he doesn't flinch. He doesn't show an ounce of emotion as he lifts his raven-hued gaze to lock on me. Fire burns in those dark and endless orbs as his lashes attempt to hide the flames.

"Now that you mention it," he ponders, his voice a whisper filled with menace. "I do quite like a woman on her knees." The promise in his words has my core pulsing, causing me to silently admonish myself for reacting to him.

"I thought so," I tell him earnestly.

"And there's nothing like feeling the warming flesh of a woman's ass as my hand spanks it. Watching the bloom of red on her pristine skin makes my cock hard. Do you like being spanked *piccola ballerina*?" The rough, husky tone of his accent trickles its way up from the base of my spine to the back of my neck, causing goose bumps to flourish on my skin.

Heat blooms on my cheeks at the question. Narrowing my gaze, I pin him with a hateful glare. "That's none of your business." Even as I spew the response, I know it's an unbidden confession that I'm not experienced in what he's asking.

Enzo chuckles, his friend joins in the amusement at my expense. "Oh, my sweet little wife, soon, every moan and whimper will be mine. And that body of yours…" He pauses for a long moment, ensuring

I'm listening, before he affirms, "Is mine."

Mario rises to his feet before tipping a salute to his boss, leaving us alone. Enzo drops his hands to his sides, and I pray he'll leave, instead, he walks toward me, causing me to retreat, only for him to follow.

"You'll stay in your bedroom today. The contract had all the given specifications of what you need for school, and I'll ensure you get it. But if you step out of line, consider all those things gone," he informs me, his tone confident.

"I'm not some unruly teenager you can set boundaries for," I bite out, but the moment I do, I realize my mistake because Enzo's hand is at my face, his fingers digging into my cheeks as he holds me steady.

"This is my house, and with you living here, you'll abide by my rules." There's a no-nonsense grit to his voice. Even if I could respond, I wouldn't, because if he takes my dancing away from me, I'll be lost. It's the only thing I love in this world. It's the only thing I have that reminds me of my mother. And I'll be damned if Enzo de Rossi takes that away from me. My heart thumps against my ribs, reminding me that even though I've angered him twice in the last two days, I'm still alive.

Barely.

I nod as much as I can, while he holds my face.

"Good girl." He offers one last wolfish grin before releasing me and turning on his heel. Once he reaches the door, he throws over his shoulder, "And don't do anything stupid." He steps out and shuts the door, but I don't hear the lock click.

Rushing to the door, I stand silently against the frame, my hand trembling as I reach for the handle. I can't hear any footsteps on the other side, and I'm almost certain he's waiting. That's why he told me not to do anything stupid, because he's expecting me to attempt an escape.

I want nothing more than to open it. But for a long while, I breathe deeply. I focus on the exercises that my dance teacher would drill into my mind, and I step back, allowing Enzo to win this one. He has complete control over my life, and I'm going to have to live with that if I want to dance.

I make my way over to the balcony door, opening it. The fresh air from the chilly morning hits me in the face, and I shiver. It's almost as if Enzo is here, touching me. But, even as I think about his hands, his fingers, I know there's no ice when we make contact.

I don't want to admit it.

Not even to myself.

But when he touches me, it burns.

ENZO

I'm ANXIOUS.

Being around her has already frustrated me, but her sassy comebacks, and the fire that flickers in her pretty green eyes, are enough to have my attention caught in her net. I know I can't love her, she's the enemy, but deep down I wonder if fucking her will get the need to see her submit, out of my system.

The afternoon sky is ablaze with bright sunshine, but the air outside is icy. The seasons are changing, and soon enough, we'll be in the middle of winter with snow coming down in sheets. This is the time of year I like to fly to Black Hollow, a small island off the Southern coast of Italy. A place I've come to love.

Maybe.

I glance up to look at Mario sitting behind the

wheel of my charcoal-hued Mercedes Benz SUV. His focus is on the road, but I know he has questions. I can see them dancing in his eyes.

I allowed him to sit with Luna. And from what I can tell, they had a fiery conversation. He hasn't told me what he said to her. I only caught the last bit of their talk, but I knew my little dancer wouldn't cower under the weight of his gaze.

He glances at me in the rear-view mirror. "So, are you going to tell me what your plan is for the girl?" His Italian accent is thick as his tongue rolls around the syllables. He's been here for a year now, coming from my hometown of Reggio Calabria in the south of Italy. We grew up together, but my folks brought me to America when I was sixteen.

Since the moment Mario arrived, I knew he had to be close because he was always my sanity when I was younger and not thinking straight. And I'm thankful for him.

"I don't know," I tell him honestly. There's no question, I must go through with the wedding, but I know that's not what he's asking. He knows me better than I do myself, and he wants my response on whether she'll take her place by my side.

There aren't any rules in our family that say I must be wed to step into the role of Boss, but I'm not sure my father would be pleased if I go back on my word. In the contract, it states she must take my last name, and she must bear my children, an heir to the Familia.

"You know, you're a bad liar, *cugino*," Mario says with a smirk. "She's gotten under your skin."

"It's not even been two days," I bite out, frustration flowing through me at the accusation. I don't want to admit it, but something tells me Mario will needle away at me until I'm confessing every damn thought I have about her. "Make sure she has the studio ready for tomorrow."

"Are you going to watch her dance?" he queries, but there's a hint of amusement in his tone which only frustrates me more. I pin him with a glare, only for him to laugh out loud, the sound echoing in the space of the car.

"You're a fucking *stronzo*, Mario." I pull out my cell phone and find a message from Valentino waiting for me. When I tap it open, my attention is caught on the order. "Take me to the warehouse," I tell Mario without looking up. I respond quickly to Valentino to let him know I'm on my way.

"What's going on?" Mario's question has me looking up with a smile on my face. It's the first one I've allowed myself to have since my little ballerina walked into my home.

"The men have brought in Olivetti," I inform my best friend. The man in question has been eluding us, but still dealing within our territory. Tonight, he'll learn nobody crosses a De Rossi. And the grin on Mario's face confirms just how much fun we're about to have.

Mario presses his foot on the gas, taking a quick left turn, only to earn himself screeching tires and blaring horns from the drivers behind him. "Sorry about that, boss," he says with a chuckle, even though I've told him repeatedly to call me by my name, he persists on the title of *boss* when we're on a job.

It doesn't take long for us to reach the warehouse. This place is owned by the De Rossi clan, and we ensure that it's in frequent use. From captives who've stolen from us to men who have sullied the family name. And there are also times when we bring in the worst of the worst—criminals who do sick shit in the world. It's our job to make sure the city is cleansed of vile human beings. And I'm the one who does the cleaning.

When we pull up into the warehouse, I push open the car door and am assaulted with an ice-cold breeze, which promises we're in for a terrible winter. Only, I enjoy the cold. It's the only time I'm able to breathe in deeply and forget the stench from the enemies I kill.

In summer, a body rots quicker, the smell is stronger, and I tend to draw out the torture, which only makes the memories more tangible in my mind. Even when I don't want them to be. Buttoning up my suit jacket, I take in the area, which is empty aside from the three cars parked beside ours. So, it's taken three of our men to get this asshole tied down.

Right on the edge of the city is a derelict warehouse that's been in my family since I can remember. My father used it when he was Underboss, and when I stepped up the ladder, he gave me the keys. Most children reach twenty-one and receive keys to a home, or a car, or some other mundane item, but I got my own torture chamber.

"Looks like they had their work cut out for them," Mario assesses, noting the blood that trails its way toward the entrance. That's a lot of crimson for a man who still needs to go through the trauma of my questioning.

The moment we reach the doorway, sounds of choking and gurgling hit me, and I step inside to find the man I'm about to torture tied to a chair. His shirt and slacks are already blood-stained, and his face is a mess.

"What the fuck is going on here?" My voice booms through the vast space. Three of our men turn to look at me, shock apparent on their faces when they realize who's walked in. Their boss, the man they're meant to fucking bow to. The Dark fucking Prince of the De Rossi clan. Each of them dressed in black, from head to toe. They're large, burly men, but their three-piece suits belie the violence that they're capable of, and that's why women drop to their knees for our soldiers.

"B-boss," one of them snivels. "We were just having some fun." His face is a picture of guilt and fear. I sneer. Good. He needs to be terrified of me because I'm not in a good mood at all.

"Fun?" I arch a brow at him, my face void of emotion, but my anger is palpable.

He nods slowly before straightening his spine. "Sorry, boss. We got a little carried away knowing what he did. We found him in an abandoned house with a young girl."

This piques my interest. "Oh? How old?"

"N-n-no I-I d-didn't d-d-do—"

"Shut. Up." My words are annunciated, so the asshole in the chair slumps lower in his seat. Blood fills his mouth from his missing teeth, which is a shame because I would've loved to have pulled them out myself. But I'll make do with the rest of him.

"Sir," one of our other men steps forward, his expression filled with confidence as he hands me his cell phone. Taking it from him, I peer down at the screen, which has my stomach twisting in knots, bile forcing its way up my throat, and I have to swallow down the acid before lifting my gaze away.

"I've seen enough." I hand him back his phone

before reaching for my blade. The knife that's been sheathed glints in the weak light that comes from the overhanging bulbs. The warehouse is nothing more than an empty shell, no closed rooms, only metal and steel.

"P-please," Olivetti begs as I near him slowly. A hunter about to slay his dinner. I stop in front of him, and his head tips back so he can watch me, but there's nothing he can say or do to stop the inevitable.

"You know," I start. "There are times I wonder about men like you." I step around the chair, trailing the tip of my knife along his shoulder, up his neck and over the edge of his ear. "Men who do vile things." My words are a whisper, but he hears them. "Men who I enjoy flaying slice by slice before watching their life drain from soulless eyes. Those are the men who make my job so much easier."

All the men who stand watching can hear me. Their rapt attention is on my movements.

They don't flinch when I nick flesh with steel. Sharp metal against wrinkled skin. There's no match for it, which is why I enjoy this so much. Leaning in, I inhale the fresh smell of blood, the metallic fragrance that's filled my nostrils since I was a young boy.

I smile.

"I think you need to learn a lesson," I inform my victim. "But before you do, you're going to tell me exactly who the fuck is selling you drugs and young girls." It's not a question, it's not even a fucking request, because he *will* give me what I need. Before he can answer, I press the tip of the blade to his ear, the sleek steel slipping easily into the shell, slowly and gently, slicing the old, tanned skin.

"I-I... P-p-please, D-De R-Rossi," he begs, only for me to push the weapon deeper into the canal where it disappears. His screams are music to my ears.

"Please?" I taunt, twisting the metal until I see blood oozing from his ear. "I think I'm being very lenient with you here," I inform him before pulling my knife from him. "I could fuck your mouth with this." I flick the weapon in front of his face, only to listen to him whimper and beg some more.

"The man isn't someone to be messed with. If I tell you—"

"I don't give a fuck what he'll do because you're dead, anyway." My words are delivered with a dark promise of what's coming. "Who are the men dealing in our territory?" I ask once more. My teeth clenched so hard, my jaw ticks.

When Olivetti doesn't answer fast enough, I sink the blade into his shoulder. Crimson spurts from the wound drenching me in his life force, which I'm about to snuff out. His scream bounces off the walls, his body cowering in agony as I twist my hand, opening him more and more with every tilt of the knife.

"I-I don't know t-the m-man g-g-giving orders," he splutters, more blood drips from his lips as he coughs up the Merlot-colored fluid. Instead of being delectable and delicious, its flavor comes from the eye-watering stench of metal.

I pull the blade from his shoulder only to lower it, sinking in the one place a man will always try to protect. The organ that makes stupid men do filthy things. "Who the fuck are you working for?"

Another agonizing cry of mercy from Olivetti, but I only smile when his watery gaze locks on mine. Guilt flickers in his dark stare, but I know it's all an act. He doesn't feel it. Not truly. Men who are ravaged by guilt don't do what he did. The photo on Frederico's phone was all the proof I needed to finish this job with a smile on my face.

"T-Tommaso Cavallone," he suddenly spews.

His confession has me straightening quickly. I'm in front of my victim within seconds, the gasps from the men who are witnessing the show ring in my ears alongside the name of the Underboss to the Cavallone clan. The same Familia of the woman I'm about to marry.

Confusion settles in my mind, and with a quick glance at Mario, I offer him a nod. He knows what it means—find Valentino. Something isn't right. But right now, I turn my focus on the bastard before me.

I don't second guess myself. I end his life with a flick of my wrist, embedding my blade into his chest, right through his blackened heart. But even as I judge this bastard, I know the thing that keeps me alive, that muscle beating in my chest, is no lighter than his.

The only difference between us is I have limits.

But when it comes to killing monsters, those boundaries disappear.

LUNA

The door slides open as the sun rises behind the house. The city is almost glinting with promises as I turn to find a woman who looks far too *motherly* to be working for a monster like Enzo de Rossi. I expected his staff to all be beautiful, statuesque, model-like creatures in small maid uniforms.

But I'm being judgmental.

"*Bella regazza*," she murmurs as she sets down a tray with a smile on her face. "Welcome to your new home." Her expression is kind, and I find myself lowering my defenses.

"*Grazie*." I return her kindness with a small curtsy, only for her to blanche at the action.

"No, you're *principessa*," she informs me. "You do not do that." She wags her finger, admonishing me. I should never have done something that stupid. I understand the way things work in a home like this, but it's the first time I've seen a friendly face.

"I'm sorry, my mistake," I whisper, making my way toward her with my hands held out. "It's okay." Even as I try to assure her, she seems worried, her brows furrowing as she regards my extended hand. And for a long moment, I pray she doesn't tell Enzo what I've done.

Even if he doesn't accept me as his partner, his queen in this Familia, I have to act like one. It may not be new to me, I've been taught from a young age what's expected of me, but there are times I wish I was *normal*.

"You will eat, then come to dance," she informs me quickly, before leaving me in the room staring at the door she's just shut. It seems my fiancé has made sure my schooling doesn't come to a halt while living in this skyscraper palace he calls home.

I'm excited to dance again.

It's been a couple of days, which is the longest I've gone without at least practicing. I tried last night, but it's just not the same without my bar. I miss it. My body needs it. As if I'm addicted to the rush of bending and pirouetting and twirling while trying to keep my focus.

Since I first put on my ballet flats at six-years-old, I knew it was something I would always love.

The music thrilled me from head to toe, transporting me to another time and place. And each year I grew older, taller, I prayed I could always dance.

And now, at eighteen, I'm thankful my constant practicing has kept me limber and I'm still able to do the one thing I love—ballet. It's the only constant that will keep me sane in my new life. And as I drink down my tea, and race to the en suite, I smile because I'm getting ready for a day of hard training.

I'm certain uncle Tommaso would have informed Enzo that I only work with one trainer. He's been with me since I was sixteen and performed in my first production of Swan Lake. And I don't know what I would do without him.

Once I'm dressed in my white tights, net skirt, and leotard that hugs my slender frame like a glove, I sigh happily. All dressed, I head out of the room to find the hallway empty. I did a little exploring, but now that I can get out of my bedroom, I venture toward the living room where I find Mario settled at the dining room table which is visible from the open plan space.

He glances up when I walk in. The corner of his mouth tilts into a wolfish grin, but there's something I can't quite put my finger on which flickers in his eyes. As if he knows something I don't.

"What are you doing here?" I ask as I stop at the sofa, not wanting to be close to him. His dark eyes lock on mine, but then he trails his gaze over me as if he's assessing me and my outfit, which has awareness skittering down my spine.

"Work." His response is cold and detached, a contrast to how he's looking at me. He doesn't make a move to come toward me, which calms me somewhat, but deep down, I know it's only for show. This man could probably move so quickly, he'd catch me before I even made it to my bedroom door.

He's trained.

A killer.

"Okay," I say before turning for the kitchen, but I stop dead in my tracks when I hear his computer lid shut with a click.

"He will never love you, but you don't have to be faithful either." He's not joking. There is no amusement on his face, and for a second, I wonder if he's propositioning me. "There are men out there willing to be discreet."

"Is that the life you think I want?" I challenge, my hands fisting at my sides as anger shoots through me at the thought of being nothing more than arm candy for the likes of the De Rossi clan. Mario doesn't respond. It's as if he's shocked at my outburst.

But then he sighs and pushes to his full six foot three inches and locks those gray eyes on me. "All I meant was that you don't have to be lonely."

"If I'm married to a man who doesn't love me, it doesn't matter whose bed I sleep in, I'll always be lonely." His brows shoot up at my words, and my chest tightens.

"You're an intelligent girl," Mario says softly when he reaches me. His expression is serious when he leans in close. His cologne is spicy, and warm reminding me of a roaring fire in the coldest of winters. I wonder why he is so warm, and yet the man I'm going to marry is so ice cold. "Maybe, just maybe, you will change him." His words take a moment to sink in, and when they do, my brows furrow.

I tip my head back, forcing myself to meet his stare. "What makes you say that?"

This time, the corners of his mouth tip upward and I'm gifted with what I can only assume is a very rare smile. "Because you're the first woman who's ever been around him that doesn't seem affected by his position in this life. Also, I quite like seeing him challenged by someone so young and pretty." Mario winks. It's a playful gesture which makes him seem younger than what I imagine him to be.

"And what if I do change him?" I ask as curiosity burns through my veins, warming me from the inside out. If I could make a man like Enzo de Rossi fall in love with me, perhaps this life my uncle has pushed me into won't be so bad.

"I'd like to see you try," Mario tells me earnestly. "You have a month before the wedding," he says. "If you can change his mind within that time, you'll not only be a queen and revered by the men of the Familia, but you'll have the adoration of someone who loves deeply."

"How can he love if he's never had a woman stay longer than one night?"

Mario laughs out loud at my question, the deep rumble vibrating through his chest. The corners of his eyes crinkling as the amusement paints his expression in lightheartedness. "Oh, sweet girl, he does love. He loved his mother and father very much. And me, I'm his best friend, and even though I'm meant to take a bullet for him within our hierarchy, he would take one for me just as quickly."

When silence hangs between us after his admission, my mind races with thoughts of perhaps changing the leader of one of the most feared families in New York. Mario's cell phone buzzes in his pocket, and when he pulls it out, his expression sobers.

"I have to go, but your dance studio is ready, and your classes start at ten," he informs me as he shoves the device back into his pocket without responding to the message. "If you need anything, the phone on the counter has been programmed with my number."

I glance over my shoulder to find the iPhone lying in wait for me. When I look at Mario again, he offers me a nod and smile before turning for the door. "Thank you," I call out to him, feeling as if I've connected with someone. This life isn't something I chose for myself, but perhaps I can make it my own.

"Any time, sweet girl," he responds before he leaves me alone in the apartment.

I ponder our conversation as I make something to eat and grab a coffee before settling at the breakfast bar. My parents always taught me to be strong in the face of adversity. I learned to defend myself at thirteen. My father thought it would be good for me to know how to be safe.

Even though I had bodyguards follow me around since I can remember, I'm not some pushover. Enzo de Rossi cannot scare me. And after my talk with Mario, confidence brims inside me as I finish up my food and tidy the kitchen.

Enzo may be the Boss, but I will make the King fall.

ENZO

"There isn't a chance in hell I'm bowing down to any fucking Irish mobster," I inform Franco Moretti. "They're nothing but animals."

Franco chuckles. He's known me most of my life, and even though he is a few years older than I am, he's still someone I can get along with. Franco took over as the Boss of the Moretti Familia when his father stepped down. He's one of the few men I know that wanted to be a leader before he turned sixteen. He made his first kill at twelve, and since then, he's delved into the darkness without guilt.

"What are we going to do about the arms coming in this weekend?" I ask, pushing the folder with the information toward him.

"I have my men setting up. We will be waiting

for them. It's not every day you get to kill fifty Irishmen." His grin is nothing short of devilish. "If you'd like to join us, perhaps we can go for a drink after to celebrate."

"I want to be right there, in the throng of it. I need to..." I allow my words to linger in the air before continuing. "Release tension."

"Is this about the pretty new girl that you have living with you?" His dark brow arches as he regards me with a smile. "I heard your father left you with a bit of a legacy to continue."

"He did. I think this was his last *fuck you* to me," I inform him with a smile. "He always told me I would get married, even though I denied it. But what makes me angry, frustrated even, is that the contract is with the Cavallones."

"I believe so. Interesting choice from Salvatore. I suppose he's ensuring their lineage ends with her. It's clever."

I can't help but laugh. "Only you would think that."

He narrows his gaze, his dark eyes trying to dig deep inside my mind. "You don't?"

"I don't know what to think. Also, I need to talk to you about Tommaso. When I was questioning Olivetti, he mentioned he'd been working for the Cavallones. My men are digging into it. Do you know anything about it?"

"I've heard whispers. Apparently, he's a man who knows what he wants. Since Tommaso is dead, thanks to your clan, I have a feeling someone is going to pop out of the woodwork. Tommaso wanted to be Boss for far too long not to have a back-up."

Franco's words hit right in my chest. Something doesn't feel right, and I can't quite put my finger on it. "I don't like it. My intuition is telling me there's much more to the contract, and to the Cavallone family than meets the eye."

"Perhaps there's someone on the inside?" Franco suggests, causing my body to stiffen. I didn't want to voice it, but that could be what's bothering me. "

"I'll start questioning tomorrow," I tell him as I ponder this idea. If we have a mole in the clan, I'll find him, and then I'll fucking kill him. But not before I make him pay for hours.

"If you need anything, let me know. I look forward to hearing what you come up with. And by the way, I can't wait to meet your woman. I've seen her around, quite the little vixen." Franco laughs when I do at his analogy. He's not interested in her. I can tell by his expression there's no desire in his eyes, but he is intrigued.

I nod slowly, wondering what to say about Luna. I didn't expect her to be so fiery, but I have a feeling my father knew it. That's possibly why he chose my fate to be linked with hers. Since I knew I would be Boss, I told him I would never marry, but even in death, my father knew what he wanted for me, and I have no choice but to obey. "She's... different." It's my final response to Franco, who chuckles.

"That's not a good thing," he says as he leans back in his chair, his hands behind his head, and he looks like he's on vacation, all that's missing is the sun and some women in bikinis waiting on us.

But he's intrigued me, so I ask, "Why?"

"When women are different, they're not good for us. We fall head over heels."

"Are you saying you were in love? You're one of the most ruthless Bosses in the world. People whisper about you from here all the way to Italy. They even in fucking murmur about you and what you've done in China."

He nods slowly. "I've allowed myself to feel something, but it didn't work out. And that's why I can say it's not safe when they're different. They tend to make you want it more."

"She's the princess of the Familia who had my father killed. There is no way in hell she will ever make me love her." My tone is filled with confidence, but the man before me who I've known most of my life only smiles.

"So," he finally says. "On Saturday, we'll meet at our warehouse, and travel together to the pier."

Back to business. "Once the job is done, we will head over to the club and enjoy a nice Scotch."

"Sounds like a plan. I want those Irish bastards to know exactly who they've fucked over." Pushing to my feet, I button my suit jacket. "I want them to know the De Rossi name, and second guess any other chances they take coming into New York."

"They will," he agrees. "Joining forces only makes us stronger. At least, for this job. If you keep to your entertainment venues and we share in the arms deals, we won't have any trouble."

"What about that club you're so in love with?" I question, knowing more about your business associates makes you formidable for two reasons—you can use the information to build a connection, or you can use it to blackmail them. With Franco, I want to build a familiar connection which will allow us to do business. It's the only club that I've had my eye on that's been difficult to pin down.

He watches me, tipping his head to the side before he smiles once more. It's a scary sight to see a man like him smile—you don't know if he's about to kill you or laugh along with you. "You really want it?"

I nod. "What's your interest in it?" I ask, my brow creasing with intrigue.

He sighs, pushing to his feet, he looks over the paperwork on the table before lifting his dark stare to mine. "The owner is a man I'd like to sort out."

I know what that means, I don't ask why, and I don't make a comment on it. If Franco has something in this deal, then perhaps once he's completed whatever plan he has, I'll be able to purchase the club. It's stunning, on the right side of town, and it will allow me to turn it into something exclusive.

"I can give you first option to purchase once it's available," he tells me as we round the table and shake hands. "Only if you promise to allow me to hire someone to work there, full time. She doesn't lose her job; she doesn't walk away."

"A woman."

"Why else do bastards like us do anything?" he challenges with a dark laugh, which I mimic because he's right. Even with our lives being filled with violence, there are always women who run the show. We just don't allow them to know that.

"See you soon," I tell him as I make my way to the elevator which takes me down to the basement. The men who have come along with me follow, and we head to the cars together. I find Mario having a smoke when I reach the SUV. "It looks like we're going to have an interesting weekend."

"Oh? Did he agree to the ambush?" He pulls deeply on the smoke, the swirl of white filling the space between us.

"He did. He also mentioned the club," I tell him.

"It's a done deal. I'll have first dibs on purchase if he can get rid of the owner. I have a feeling there's more to the story than meets the eye. I'm going to look into it."

"I can do that for you, Boss," Mario says, a sideways smile on his face.

We slide into the cars and head out. "Did Valentino confirm the meeting?"

Mario nods in response before he tells me, "He did. Tomorrow morning. Apparently not everyone could make tonight."

"Take me back to the apartment. It's time I spent a few hours with my fiancée. She needs to learn about her future husband." I inform him before settling back and pulling out my phone. There are few emails I respond to, but my mind is on what I'm about to find when I step into the house. If she's still dancing, I'll watch from my office. When I had the cameras set up around the studio, I knew I would not be able to work from home if there was something important, I needed to do.

One thing I can say for certain, is that Luna Cavallone is going to be my distraction for long time to come. Perhaps fucking her out of my system is the way to go. But the scent of her perfume—candied apples—makes me rethink that plan.

Last night was something else. Feeling her tremble beneath me made every nerve in my body spark with electricity and desire. I wanted to taste her. To throw her on the bed and spread those lithe legs and see what she's hiding. I wonder briefly if she's a virgin. I open my email once more and pull up her medical records.

She's been to see a doctor a handful of times in her life. Nothing serious. Just the usual. She's had her wisdom teeth removed, and she's only just gone on the pill. The date indicates she got it just before her eighteenth birthday, which has me wondering if she's no longer a virgin.

That thought has jealousy surging through me and I have to shake it off because even the thought of another man's hands on her fuels my rage. I'm not usually a jealous person, but right now, knowing she's mine, I can certainly kill any other man who touches her.

"I want more background on Luna," I tell Mario quickly without looking up from my phone. "I want everything there is to know. The documents her uncle sent aren't well researched."

"I'll get on it."

"I want ex-boyfriends, any teachers that may have wanted her, I want to know everything right down to the moment she got her first period." My order is met with silence which has me looking up from the screen to find Mario's stare in the rearview mirror. "What?"

"Is someone finally coming to terms with the fact that he's about to get married?" he taunts, and if he weren't sitting in the front, I would've probably broken his nose in frustration.

"Shut up." I shove my phone away as we pull into the garage. I'm out of the car and in the elevator without waiting for him. At times, he knows me far too well. He can read me like a book.

The metal car takes me to the penthouse. The doors whoosh open, and I step out into my private hallway. Thiago and Adriano glance over at me and smile.

"What's going on?" I ask.

Thiago is the one who answers, "Nothing, Boss. Been a quiet day. She did offer us something to drink. Nice girl." My hands fist at my sides, but I swallow down the jealousy. This is fucking ridiculous.

"I trust she's still inside?"

"Yes, boss," Adriano affirms with a nod.

Ignoring them, I step into my apartment and the music hits me as the speakers blare out a song. I recognize the tune, but instead of a male singing, a woman's melodic tone greets me. *Shameless* by Sofia Karlberg fills the space and I wonder just what my little dancer is doing.

I make my way toward the studio which is on the second floor of the penthouse. The glass doors offer no privacy, and I lean against the door frame, my arms folded as I take in the pretty dancer pirouetting around the smooth floorboards.

She's not just a dancer listening to the music. She *feels* it. It's how her body moves that shows it and I can't believe this is a woman I hate. And I do. But perhaps it's because of her last name, not necessarily because of her.

Her body is encased in soft pinks, her hair loose instead of being bound tightly at the back of her head, and she stops spinning before moving into a few flowing movements which showcase her beautiful hourglass figure.

My zipper becomes tighter as I watch. The skirt she's wearing lifts showing off her pert ass and her shapely thighs as she moves. The teacher I hired, a woman, stands at the front of the room, watching Luna. She doesn't notice me at first, but when she does, her eyes widen, and I press my finger to my lips, indicating she should be quiet and not interrupt my little dancer.

For a long while, I just stand and watch Luna, mesmerized by the way she moves. Obsession. It's a sickness she's brought upon me. And I want to make her pay. Before she arrived, I was convinced hurting her would be the plan, but the effect she has on me has me wondering if it would be better to make her fall by showing her love and affection. Making sure she loves me and then breaking her, leaving her alone in the world.

But then I recall last night. When I had her pinned up with my hand, she whimpered so beautifully. It was a siren's song. My cock agrees. She doesn't want soft, gentle touches. No. My little dancer wants me to bruise that smooth porcelain skin.

Suddenly, the silence greets us with a deafening thud, and my gaze locks on the girl in question. She offers a strangely shy smile, as if I've caught her doing something she shouldn't be doing. Her cheeks are a soft rosy hue, and my cock throbs against my pants when I think about making sure her ass is just as red. At eighteen, she's younger than what I would have chosen for my wife. But as I look at her curves, how she carries herself, I realize she's grown up quickly.

She's had to.

In this life, in our world, there isn't time to be childish and playful.

You either sink or swim.

And my little dancer can swim with the sharks.

LUNA

He stands there watching me as if I were on a stage. There's a slight smile on his lips. My heartbeat is a wild animal in my chest as I watch Enzo. He makes no move to walk into the room, but instead, waits patiently at the doorway.

His shirt is still pristine, his jacket is unbuttoned. I know he had a meeting, and thankfully, I was able to concentrate on my classes today instead of being nervous with him in the apartment with me.

"Luna," the sound of Violetta's voice startles me, and I jump. "We're done for the day." She offers me a smile before taking her personal belongings and leaving me with Enzo. It doesn't calm my heartbeat, and the silence is deafening as I stand aimlessly in the middle of my studio.

When Mario told me he had one decorated for me, I expected a room with a few beams, but what I found instead was breath taking. The walls are all mirrored, the floor is made up of smooth wooden panels that make it easy to practice on. The ceiling is lit with fluorescent lights, which can be dimmed, if need be, and the speakers that surround the studio are of the utmost quality.

"What are you doing here?"

My question seems silly when he laughs. The sound is a deep rumbling vibration that makes my stomach do somersaults. He seems happy today. Better than he was last night. Each time I recall what happened, my body tenses. Not in fear, but something else I don't want to put my finger on, because if I do, I'll only admit what I want and feel.

"I live here," he informs me in a tone that is filled with amusement. I don't know what's changed since the sun rose this morning, but it seems to have lightened his mood.

It's strange to see a man like him in a good mood. A mafia king—ruthless and volatile—grinning like a schoolboy on Christmas. "I just meant... I thought you were at a meeting."

"I was. And then I came home. I didn't realize I needed your permission to do so," he says before toeing off his shoes and stepping onto the wooden floorboards. His socks—black as night—cover his feet, and I wonder what he looks like naked. The thought rushes into my mind with embarrassment burning my cheeks.

"You don't," I choke out when I look up to find him inches from me. He reaches for me, and I can't stop myself from flinching. His tender touch burns me when his fingertips come into contact with my chin, and he tips my head back further. I'm not sure what he's doing, but when his hand wraps around my throat, I realize he's looking for bruises where his fingers were last night.

I covered up the soft blues and purples, but not before I ran my fingers along them myself. That was the moment I realized the twisted thoughts in my mind have rooted themselves deep inside me. The way he marked me warmed my belly, and instead of scaring me, the way it should have, my core throbbed at the dark images that took hold of me.

"You look pretty," Enzo murmurs suddenly, his voice dropping to a gravelly baritone that scrapes itself along my flesh. "So, fucking beautiful with my hand on you," he continues, and every utterance only seems to have my thighs squeezing together and my nipples hardening against my tight bodysuit.

Shit.

"Let go of me," I bite out, forcing my anger to the forefront of my mind and shoving the desire for his touch to the back. I can't do this. I can't *want* him.

This is a man with Cavallone blood on his hands. His family killed my father. Although I can't judge him since my father was a murderer too, I won't allow myself to fall into the trap that so many other women have.

I need to remember Enzo de Rossi is the enemy.

My plan to make him love me needs to be my focus, and the only way I'm going to do that is to be stronger than he is. The higher someone climbs, the harder they'll fall, and he's at the top now. The only way is down. And I'll make sure of it.

Finally, he releases his hold on me and shakes his head. When he turns his back to me, I cross my arms over my chest to hide my nipples that are now small peaks against the soft pink fabric. I don't want him to see the effect he has on me.

"Are you enjoying the class?" he asks without facing me. "They've told me Violetta is the best," he continues before I can answer his first question. I want to ask him why he didn't hire my trainer, Adriano, but I don't bother because I have a feeling that he preferred a woman alone with me.

"Yes, she's good. It was nice to be able to dance again." My voice is a whisper. Before Enzo turns, I pull on my hoodie and let out a breath so I can focus on him being the bad man and me being his prisoner.

"You're exquisite," he tells me suddenly, causing

my heart to leap into my throat. *He was watching me.* I wonder how long he was standing there before the music stopped.

My cheeks burn as he regards me with those dark eyes that seem to dig through my soul, trying to find something I can't offer him. I cannot tell him what my trump card is, because once I play it, it will ensure he won't kill me. "Thank you."

"It's not the first time I've seen you dance," he admits, still with his back to me. I wonder if he finds it easier not to look at my face while talking, while confessing his sins. And I wonder how many sins I can get him to admit to.

"Where have you watched me?" I ask, as I pad over to the bar. I hold on to the metal, untying my shoes. Instead of looking at his back, I glance in the mirror, finding his reflection. His profile is that of a tortured man. It's strange. Usually he's so confident, but right now, he looks like he's in pain.

His hands fist at his sides. He doesn't move for such a long time that I wonder if he's ever going to speak again. But then he does, and it knocks the breath from my lungs. "I've spent the past three years watching you, waiting for my moment. When the war first started between our families, I bought every theater in New York, and I planned to buy every theater in every city you would eventually dance in."

His admission has a gasp escaping my lips. I'm frozen in place. My mind races through the words he's just uttered, but they make no sense to me. He doesn't know me. He didn't know me. Surely, I was nothing more than a stranger to him until he learned of the contract. "What?"

This time, he looks at me.

A man possessed. Obsessed.

"You've become something of an addiction for me. As if I can't turn away when you're on the stage. As if you've lured me like a goddamned siren," he tells me, and it shouldn't make my stomach flip-flop with excitement, but it does. "An obsession." Most boyfriends and fiancés buy their women flowers and write poems to them. Mine tells me I'm his obsession.

I'm speechless.

All I can do is watch him. There's nothing to say to what he just told me. I don't know how to feel about it. Maybe, just maybe, my plan will work. There is a fine line between love and obsession, and perhaps I can push Enzo over it. Maybe I can distort the desire in his eyes, and I can make him feel more.

"Don't take this as me confessing my love for you," he says, as if reading my mind. He closes the distance between us quickly. "There is nothing I hate more than a Cavallone," he informs me coldly.

I lean back, my eyes on his. "And what happens

when I become a De Rossi?" I challenge. They say never to poke a sleeping bear, but I've always loved a challenge. But the hatred that burns in his eyes makes me wish I could swallow back what I've just said.

The sneer on Enzo's face is nothing short of poisonous. "You may take my name, but you will never have the blood of a De Rossi in your veins," he threatens, causing my heart to drop to my stomach. My lungs struggle to work, to pull in much needed air.

It shouldn't hurt so much.

I don't love this man.

I don't even *like* him.

Then why does my chest feel so tight when his words hit me there?

"I wouldn't want your blood in my veins, even if I were dying," I bite back as anger takes hold of me. But if I had to truly admit it, I'm trying to hurt him as much as he hurt me. But it doesn't work because he only laughs. The sound bouncing off the mirrors, reflecting at me as my cheeks burn with shame.

He says nothing more, and I don't challenge him again because I'm afraid if I do, I'll break down and that's not what I want him to see. Instead, I hold my head up high, even though I'm clearly defeated in this war between us.

"Tonight, you'll dine with me, and wear

something respectable," he tells me coolly once he's done and leaves me in the studio like nothing more than an afterthought.

My eyes burn as tears brim behind my lashes. I don't blink. I don't allow myself to cry because if I do, I'll never stop. Perhaps my plan will fail. Maybe I'm not strong enough to make the king fall. Maybe I'm nothing more than a lost princess.

ENZO

To say that I've hidden in my office since I left Luna in the studio would be an understatement. I watched her crying on the small screen. The camera focused on the soft way her lower lip trembled, how she gripped the steel bar trying to appear strong.

She's fragile.

Which means she can break.

I can't stop the smile from forming on my lips.

I kept the cameras on for a while after she'd gone to her bedroom in case she returned.

She didn't.

I'm sure she's getting ready for this evening's dinner. I cannot wait to see what she wears.

My phone rings and I notice Mario's name on screen. As I settle into my seat and flick the cameras off, I answer. "What can you tell me?"

"I've just emailed you everything we could dig up on your *wife*," he tells me. I can hear the amusement in his voice, which grates on my nerves. I'm staring at the two black screens which look back at me.

"I would say thank you if I didn't want to kill you," I inform Mario, only to earn a chuckle in response.

"If you killed me, you wouldn't have a best friend that would die for you," he throws back easily, and I can hear the smile in his voice. But I can't deny he's right, so I don't respond. "I have one request though," he says.

"Oh?" Mario has been with me for years, and has never asked for anything before, so for him to even mention it, must be important. "You know I'd do anything for you. Within reason."

"I know." He goes silent and for a moment I think the line has died, but then he sighs. "My brother wants to attend Black Hollow," he says.

"I don't see a problem with him doing that," I tell him. "It's a place where he can learn this life, as well as get a good education. Your brother can get a degree in anything he wishes."

But then Mario admits to what the problem really is. "I don't want him in this life. I never have." I understand his side of it, but I also get the need for his brother to walk in the path of those who came before.

"If you wanted to do this, spend your life being by my side and your father told you not to, would you have listened? I understand why you don't want him to take the oath, but if we're around him, keeping him safe, I don't see why he can't be a soldier."

"If I had a choice, I may not be here, Enzo. Not because I wouldn't do anything for you, or the family, but there are times I wish my life was different. Like Thiago. Even though he runs the London outfit, he's allowed to live his life differently." His words hit me right in the chest. All this time I thought Mario was happy, and now that I know he's not, I want to do something about it.

Most times, I shut off my feelings and emotions. They don't have a place in this life, but for my best friend, I open that box and rummage around to make sure he's happy.

"Then go to London," I tell him, even though I pray with everything I am, to a God who hasn't been there for me for a very long time, that he refuses to leave.

"What?" Shock is clear in Mario's voice, but with it, is hurt. Perhaps he didn't expect me to say that, but he must know I would do anything for him.

"I'm serious." I push to my feet. "I want you to

be happy. You're my best friend, and even though I would hate to lose you as my right hand, your life shouldn't be dictated by me."

"You're my Boss."

He's right. My father would roll in his grave right now if he knew what I just told Mario to do. Valentino stood by my father's side for years. Perhaps they had this exact conversation early on, but my father would never have given his friend a choice like this.

"Yes, I am." Stopping at the window which overlooks the city, I shove my hand in my pocket and pull out the watch that Mario gave me for my birthday when I turned twenty-one. That was twelve years ago. *Jesus, time flies.* I smile at the pun. "But, it's your decision, and I won't hate you for it. I won't have you killed. And I promise, I'll live even if you're not around to take a bullet for me."

Mario chuckles with me at the last sentiment. I never had a brother. Being an only child is lonely. It's a life I wouldn't wish on anyone. Perhaps that's why the Familia means so much to me. I needed connection, and with Mario, it was always there for me.

"I can't leave you," he tells me finally, and I let out the breath I've been holding. Relief washes over me. It's selfish to want him to stay, but I never claimed to be a good person. "Firstly, the moment I walk out, you'll be in danger, and I don't trust any other man to watch your back."

When he's silent, I ask, "And secondly?"

"Well, someone has to stop you from killing the poor girl," he whispers conspiratorially. *Asshole.* "She's a good person."

"Too good for me," I admit what I've been thinking since my brief encounter with her earlier. "I don't know what my father was thinking when he drew up this damn contract. It wasn't revenge, that much I can tell you."

"What? You think he did this just to torture you in his absence?"

I nod. "Of course he did. You know how much he always used to tell me I would marry one day, even when I denied it repeatedly. But I miss him," I confess in a whisper. "I know how to run the family, but I don't know how to live without his advice."

I've never once admitted this to anyone. Not even Mario. If people see any weakness in a Boss, they'll take advantage of it, and my reputation is not something I'm willing to toy with.

"I know. I get it, but you can do this. You have an army backing you," he informs me confidently. "And you have a woman who is strong enough to put up with you," he tacks on afterward.

"Speaking of which, it's time you fuck off. I need to have dinner with said woman," I say, hoping to lighten the mood.

I don't talk about emotions, but the thought of losing Mario after losing my father conjure up those feelings. I shove them back in the box, lock it up tight, and school my features as I hang up and stalk toward the dining room.

The table is set for two. Wine glasses are already filled with a supple red, and our plates are piled with dinner. The food smells delicious. All that's missing is my fiancée.

I settle at the head of the table facing the rest of the apartment. The penthouse isn't home, it's merely a hideout in the city. While the house my parents owned, where I grew up, stands empty, I spend my time here.

One day perhaps I'll show Luna the house that will forever be tarnished for me. We both lost people we loved. We're both alone, if not for each other. The realization hits me hard, but I shake it off. She doesn't deserve kindness. If it wasn't for her father starting a war, we wouldn't be in this position.

I focus on my wine, picking up the long-stemmed glass before bringing it to my lips. The lush alcohol coats my tongue and I savor the flavor as it hits my tastebuds. And that's when Luna walks in. Over the rim of my glass, a vision assaults me, and once again, I'm speechless.

Draped over her body is fabric the color of

sparkling champagne. The glittering dress hugs her curves like a second skin. Her porcelain skin a beautiful contrast to the golden material. When she steps toward me, her left leg appears through the ankle to thigh slit. Her heels are thin, straps of glinting gold. Everything about her shines, and then she offers me a smile.

"Is this respectable enough for you?" Her brow arches as she regards me through long dark lashes. Her shoulders squared, her spine straight, and her chin tipped in defiance.

I want to smile. I want to laugh, but I don't give her the satisfaction of such a reaction. Instead, I rove my gaze over her, taking her in from head to toe, and back to those olive-green orbs that pierce right through me. It's as if she's trying to find a man behind the mask, but she won't be able to because there isn't one. Not anymore, not for her.

"Sit." I turn away from her and focus on my plate. Lifting the silver dome which covers my dinner, I set it aside, and mimic the motion with her plate as well. When she doesn't obey me, I glance at her once more. "I don't like repeating myself."

"And I don't like being treated like an object, like a subservient child," she bites out, hands on her shapely hips, her mouth pursed in frustration. "If you cannot acknowledge me, then I'll eat in my room. Alone."

"You look lovely," I say, my voice barren of any emotion. "Now sit."

Slowly, ever so fucking slowly, she pulls the chair out and slips into it. Beside me, I can smell those candied apples, and it once again attempts to hit me right in the chest, reminding me of happier times. But I pick up my wine and swallow back a mouthful, allowing the scent of merlot to fill my nostrils.

"This looks nice," Luna remarks in a whisper as she picks up her fork to stab at the pasta. I wonder if she's imagining me, allowing the fork to pierce flesh. When I don't respond, she looks up, her gaze flickering with calm, with something akin to comfortable emotion.

"I've hired a private chef to prepare only the best meal for this evening."

"And you trust someone else cooking for you?" Her question gives me pause. "My father didn't allow anyone but my mother to cook. When she died, I had to do it." Sadness laces her tone, and I want to pull her into my lap and soothe her pain.

"Eat your food. I don't need to hear about your bastard of a father," I bite out before refilling my glass. Her mouth pops open as I watch her from over the rim of the crystal goblet. But she says nothing. Instead, she does as I asked and eats her meal without uttering another word.

But what she doesn't realize is that I watch every movement she makes.

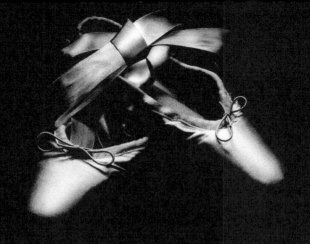

LUNA

Silence.

He seems to enjoy it, but only around me, I'm sure.

With it just being us in the apartment, there aren't any noises. Not even the bustle of the traffic reaches the double-glazed windows up here. I'm sure they're bulletproof as well. It feels as if we're sitting in a glass cage with noise canceling headphones on.

I can feel his burning gaze on me, watching me intently. But I don't meet those dark eyes because they seem to burrow into me, digging, scraping at me, wanting to know my secret. I only have one. The most important thing I hold close to my heart. At least, that's what I tell myself as I finish my dinner. Upon the last bite, I pick up my wine and sip down the last few drops before setting the glass down.

Laying my hands on the table, I sit back and look out at the city that glints before me. Twinkling stars in a city that never sleeps.

"You're welcome to go back to your room now."

Anger surges through me. "Is that what this marriage is going to be?" Snapping my glare on him, I narrow my eyes watching his expression turn from calm to something akin to rage.

"I never wanted this. You are a punishment from my father. His last dying wish was for me to marry you, to kill off the Cavallone line. I never refused my father. He was not just my parent, he was my Boss." His voice is clipped, void of emotion, but his eyes are as expressive as ever. They tell me everything he's feeling. And it's no longer anger at me, it's pain at losing the man he looked up to.

I want to fight back. I want to throw an insult at him and his family, but I know what it's like to lose your parents. So, instead of responding, I nod and push my chair away from the table. Silently, I rise to my feet and offer him a small smile. "Thank you for dinner, it was lovely." I turn and make my way to the bedroom, where I'll stay until he leaves for work in the morning. At least, I pray he will.

I'd like some time alone, and with him being out of the apartment, I can think about how I'm going to change his mind about me. Deep down, I realize

Enzo hates my family, not me specifically. And on top of that, he's heartbroken.

It's the same pain I felt when I lost my dad. He was my hero. In my eyes, he will always be that, even though I know he's done some unspeakable things. Sighing, I slip the sleeves of my dress down my arms and shimmy out of the soft fabric. It whooshes to the floor in a heap at my feet just as my bedroom door opens.

Spinning around, I almost topple as the material binds at my ankles. Within seconds, Enzo is there, his arm wrapped around my waist, his body cocooning me, and his hot breath fanning gently over my face. His lips are inches from mine as he leans over me, holding me up. Everything south of my belly button tightens when my palms land on his chest, and I feel the muscles under his dress shirt tensing.

"Be careful," he orders, his tone gravelly, husky with desire as it dances in his dark eyes. His hand is still splayed on my back as he grips me in his harsh hold, and yet I wouldn't want to be anywhere else. When he straightens, he pulls me with him before releasing me.

"Thank you." It's only then that the realization hits me. I'm standing before him in my white lace panties and matching strapless bra. I want to cover up, to wrap myself in the golden material at my feet, but I don't. Instead, I stand tall, just like I learned in class since I was six and look directly at the man before me.

It's like going head-to-head with your fate. You're unsure of what's about to happen, but there's nothing you can do to stop it. You can only hope and pray that the aftermath is not fatal.

"When you're around me, there will be no mention of your family, or my family, for that matter. We will talk about nothing more than how your day was, what you'd like to do after your classes are finished for the year, and how you can contribute to this home."

"I'm not a maid. I'm here to stand beside you," I inform him. "I know men in this life aren't particularly fond of women, but I grew up around violence, and I will not run when I face danger."

Enzo's mouth tips into a sinister grin as he reaches behind him, and before he does it, I know what's about to happen. His hand appears, and the familiar steel blade comes into view. "Aren't you scared?" he challenges before taking a step toward me. I don't want to move, but on instinct, I do. I move back slowly as he makes his way forward.

Back.

Forward.

Back.

Forward.

Back.

My heart catapults into my throat when my back hits cool glass. Enzo tips his head to the side, his gaze locking on mine as he lifts the steel blade to my nose. Lightly, ever so fucking lightly, he touches me. Goose bumps flourish as the weapon trails gently over my cheek, down to my neck where he stops, just below my ear, right on my pulse point.

Dark eyes burn with volatile amusement as he watches my erratic pulse. The thrumming in my ears is so loud, I'm certain he can hear it. He doesn't speak, he merely inhales me, as if he's smelling the fear that's emanating from me.

My hands are flat against the window. If we weren't up so high, I'm sure people would be able to see my bare backside pressed against the glass.

"What are you doing?" My whisper is scratchy against my throat, and I wonder if he can hear me. If he can hear just how nervous I am. There's a fine line between fear and nerves. And I'm teetering right on the edge.

"I want to see how *not* scared you are of me," he informs me. His expression giving nothing away. He could so easily slit my throat right here. He'd have the revenge he wants. And he wouldn't even blink. He'd have a clean-up crew walk in, tidy up the mess, and walk back out.

"I'm *not* scared of you," I tell him. My confession causes him to press into my flesh, heat courses through me, skittering down my spine, my stomach knots, tightening with every nudge of the sharp tip. But what I don't expect is the rest of my reaction. The way my thighs squeeze together, and just how my core throbs at the sting of pain.

Enzo doesn't miss a beat. His gaze tracks my movements. He knows what this does to me. The realization is shimmering in his amused stare. "Does this make my little dancer wet?" he asks, the words a whisper along my lips.

I don't respond. I can't answer him because if I do, he'll hear it in my voice. He'll pick out the need racing through my veins, heating me from the inside out. He lifts his head once more, snapping those dark eyes to me.

Inches. That's all that separates our mouths now. If he were to lean forward just a fraction, he'd kiss me.

Would he?

Do I want him to?

The answer to the latter is a resounding yes.

I want this man. Even though I would love to see him dead, my core pulses once more when he trails the blade, scraping it along my neck, down between my breasts. It's hard enough to feel the sharpness, but it's not enough to cut through my skin. He's not drawing blood, he's marking me.

He pulls the knife away suddenly, before

leaning in and brushing the shell of my ear with his lips. The heat of his breath causes a shiver to wrack through me. "I think you like this. That pretty, little cunt is wet right now because it wants a bad man to make it drip. It craves a bad man to stretch it out. And perhaps if you're a good girl, this bad man right here," he tips the knife to his chest, before delivering his final threat, "will give you exactly what you want." His words send waves of pure need crashing right to my core.

"Fuck you, De Rossi," I spit as anger blinds me. Embarrassment floods my cheeks, heat burns them, and I'm certain they're bright red. My hands land on his chest and I push him away, needing air, needing not to inhale his masculine scent. Everything about him is darkness, and even his cologne which reminds me of a hot summer night surrounds me, even when he puts much needed space between us.

"One day, little dancer," he informs me as he sheaths his blade and turns for the door. "If you behave, perhaps we can go out tomorrow." He stops at the door, his watchful glare pinning me to the window without him touching me. He exudes dominance. He wears it like his thousand-dollar suits.

But my brain doesn't seem to be linked to my mouth when I blurt, "Like, outside?" The moment the words escape me, I want to pull them back. I sound like an imbecile, just because he's made me feel things I don't want to admit to.

"Yes, Luna," he says. "Outside." And then he's gone, and I'm left to ponder what just happened. Once again, his violence turned me on. It forced me to admit, even if only to myself just what I want and need from him.

Those things he said, were true.

I do enjoy it. I do want it. And I do crave it.

But there's one thing my future husband doesn't know about me, and I'll keep it a secret right up until I can't anymore.

And the moment he finds out, I doubt I'll be useless to him anymore.

ENZO

Noise.

I don't like it.

I've always been averse to listening to a man beg for his life. Yes, I enjoy it for what it's worth, a bastard getting his comeuppance, but right now, my mind isn't in the job. I have a meeting in an hour, the first one I'll run as Boss of the Familia. The asshole before me is nothing more than a bug under my shoe.

Leaning in, I pierce his lip with the tip of my blade, while clamping his mouth shut with a pair of pliers. Blood spurts from the wound. "You've made a mess on my shoes," I inform him, my tone ice cold, venomous. "I don't like a mess."

He can't answer me with words, so all I get

are mumbles and whimpers. My anger comes from last night's interaction with Luna, rather than the criminal sitting in the chair before me, but I don't let anyone in on what's racing through my mind. I shove my hand forward, which slices through his lips, causing them to split like a snake's tongue.

"I don't like people who lie to me. If you can't give me the truth, then be sure that the next part of your body this slides through will be your tongue. You'll walk out of here half a man when I'm done with you." My threat is delivered and has the desired effect because he starts talking.

Rankin.

A man who has been undercover in the Cavallone clan for years. And now he is my prisoner. He starts confessing quickly, "I wanted to climb the ranks quickly," he tells me. "I needed to get the information before they pulled me from the job."

"And you decided that working as a fixer would be your safest bet?" I challenge as I tug on his shirt, pulling him closer to me.

He tries to shake his head, but can't because I have him in my hold. "I d-don't... I mean, t-t-there was one o-o-option to climb up to a Capo status," he admits, his voice quivering with every word.

"So, you fucked over my Familia so you could turn Capo?" I challenge, pressing harder on the pliers which I know will soon rip his lip from his face. The image the thought conjures makes me smile, which seems to confuse the man before me. "Answer me." The order is clear. "What did they make you do?" I already know the answer, but I want him to say it. I want to hear it from the horse's mouth.

"I-I-I w-w-was meant t-to k-kill y-your p-parents." The words are muffled, strained, but I heard him. This was the man that Cavallone bastard hired to murder my parents. To break my family apart. What they didn't bank on was my father having plans in place if ever something happened to him. And as much as Luna frustrates me, she is mine now. "B-but I-I d-d-didn't w-wield the w-weapon." His stutter confirms what I had suspected. He may have been there, but there was someone else holding the blade, and I'm certain that man is Tommaso Cavallone.

"I want a name," I bite out, my teeth gritting with frustration as I lean in closer, my face in his. "Tell me his name."

"T-T-Tommaso." The confession of a man with nothing left to lose. He knows he will never receive my mercy. He has no reason to lie.

"This is what happens when you fuck over a De Rossi," I inform the man in the chair before I trail my knife to his chest, and slowly, ever so torturously, cut into his flesh the D, and the R of my last name. Pride at my handiwork courses through me when

I straighten. I'm about to head into a meeting with my soldiers, with the Capos who work for me, and I'll be splattered with the blood of the man who murdered our leader.

"Clean this up," I order as I wipe my blade on the material of his discarded shirt. I turn to find Mario watching me intently. He's not at all bothered at what I just did. It's not the first man I've killed, and it won't be the last. "Let's go."

He follows behind me silently, but the thoughts racing through his mind are loud and clear. His brother wants to walk into this life. He wants a part of the violence and bloodshed, but I have feeling he's only doing it because he wants to be near Mario.

Once I'm in the back of the car, Mario starts the engine, and pulls out of the lot. He doesn't say anything until we're on the road. "I don't want him to live this life."

"I know." I can't deny, if I had a young brother who wanted this, I would also fight him tooth and nail, but there comes a time in everyone's life where they must make their own choices. You can't be guided forever. At some point, we've all got to grow up, we have to become our own person. "But he is over eighteen."

"And by the time we were that age, we both had been in this life for far too fucking long," Mario throws back, the truth hitting me in the gut. For a long moment, I wonder if Luna has seen what I have. She's grown up with a father who was a Boss. She was surrounded by soldiers and Capos since she was a baby. *Is that why she's so blasé about me?* As if I'm not scary enough for her.

"She's stronger than you think she is," Mario says, snapping me out of my reverie long enough to chuckle at my shocked expression. "She's getting to you, Boss," he tells me. "And for some reason, I quite like it."

"Why? Because you think I'm going to suddenly fall in love with her?" I challenge, frustration ebbing through me, a river of annoyance at my best friend. I don't want him to see how much she affects me, but I'm already distracted. I've never allowed anything to detract me from the job, but with Luna, I'm not myself.

"Because it's nice to see my best friend is human."

I can't respond. There are no words to throw back at him—not in anger, not in frustration, and most certainly not in agreement. The last time I was human was when I was twelve. A child, nothing more than an innocent where I believed my father was a good man and that happiness would follow me forever.

That ended quickly.

Not long after, I realized life, *this life*, is nothing

more than a fight for survival. If you don't make them fear you, you'll end up dead. And I don't want to die. No matter how much my life may feel heavy. It doesn't matter how much sorrow and heartbreak I endure. I won't give up. I will not let the enemy win.

At least my father left me with one good thing—my strength.

"Being human means that you have flaws," I inform Mario with my focus on the passing lights that skitter by. I wanted an early meeting, but as the darkness descends, I feel more at peace.

"Oh, you have flaws, Boss," Mario tells me with a chuckle. "We all do. That's why we're alive. You cannot live without the bastards." The amusement in his tone has the corners of my mouth tipping upward, but I keep my face turned so he can't see I'm smiling.

"Do you think he would be happy with this?" I ask quietly, my mind wandering to my father. He was a master at being a leader. He knew what to do, when to do it, and how to do it. Deep down, my doubt settles like a lead weight in my gut. I don't believe I can live up to his name, even though we share blood.

"Of course," Mario says finally. "You were always going to be here, sitting at the head of the table." The confidence in his tone has me finally turning to glance at him in the rear-view mirror.

"There is no doubt in anyone's mind that you're the right man to step up to the plate."

He may think that. Others may think that, but I doubt it. Yes, I was always next in line, but only by blood. I worked for years as the Familia's fixer, making sure that those who didn't pay, those who went against our code, and those who stole from us pay in blood. And as much as I know my father was happy with my work, there was always this niggling in the back of my mind that I just didn't come up to par with what he wanted.

"The reading of the last will and testament is coming up," I tell Mario. "I delayed it because I didn't want to know what he thought of me."

"You can't delay it forever," he says. "At some time, you have to come to terms with your position within the clan. You also have to admit that you are now our Boss." He's right, I have to. I wish my mind would play along. "If you show doubt to anyone else, they could use it against you."

Nodding, I turn away again as we pull up to the office block where De Rossi Incorporated is housed. The company my father started. When I learned about the contract, about Luna Cavallone, I bought every theater in the city, in the country, and smiled because I knew I could see her anytime I wanted. Watching her from the shadows became my pastime, and I reveled in it. I exit the vehicle as the rest of the men pull up and flank me.

Silently, we move into the building, taking the elevator to the top floor. When I walk into the boardroom, I find my Capos, all five of them, along with Valentino, my father's Consigliere, who I no longer need. The problem is, I think he knows it.

Mario will step in as my advisor and Valentino will be retired. He will be able to step away from the day to day running of the clan, but I don't think he will go without a fight.

"Gentlemen," I greet while unbuttoning my jacket, the bloodstains visible on my crisp white shirt. Thankfully, my undershirt is still clean. The maid will get the stains out, but not without some work. "Thank you for making the time for this meeting."

Valentino pipes up quickly, "I think we need to vote who will step up into the leader role next," he says, his eyes flicking to me, then to the rest of the men.

There's a murmur around the room as I settle in my father's chair. "I think that is a moot point, Valentino." Mario slips into the seat at my right hand, and I notice the flinch of the older man when I lean back in the chair. "My father's will is still something we need to sort out. The reading will take place in a couple of days, and then we'll know what major changes will take place, however, I am the logical successor to my father's seat."

"I agree," Carlo, one of the Capos says with a confident nod.

"Same here," this comes from Vito, who has been with the family for almost forty years. He's the eldest and is still going strong even at his age. "We have to go by the rule of the clan. We can't be changing things up now." As the oldest, he's also the one who knows the rules of being in this life better than any one of us.

"I just think that we should be progressive in our future," Valentino murmurs, but I can read his frustration at the men who support me. The other three are silent, but they nod when I glance at them.

"What about you?" I ask, taking in each one as they sit around the table.

"I agree with Carlo," Bennie says, who's the second eldest member. He became a Made Man when he was only seventeen. He took the oath of Omertà when he was still a teenager. "We don't change rules when it suits us."

The rest of the men don't respond. So, it is two who stand with Valentino, and the three with me. Which means, even if we took a vote, we'd be tied. Three for three. Mario cannot vote, because he'll side with me, and I doubt my father's advisor is going to allow it anyway.

"We will wait on the reading of will," I say

finally. "In the meantime, I want us to watch our backs. The Cavallone haven't given up, and they won't until they're all dead."

"What about the shipment coming in on Saturday?" Carlo questions. It's the main reason I called this meeting.

"I spoke with Franco Moretti. He's given us an in to join them to intercept." I glance around the room before continuing. "They'll work with us on this, and I think it's best we have the numbers, because I have a bad feeling."

"So, we're doing something because you have a *bad feeling*?" Valentino's voice cuts through the discussion, and it grates on my nerves. I flick a glare at him, arching a brow waiting for him to continue. "I just think that if you had the experience, we'd be going in guns blazing to ensure these bastards don't try this again."

"If there is one thing I've learned from my father," I bite, causing him to flinch. "It's that revenge is taken slowly. We have numbers, we have men who can fight, so I don't know why you're so concerned. I will not lose any more men from our family because of bullshit going down. We do this as I say, or you can stay at home."

The finality in my words has him sitting back. His arms folded across his chest, and I know I've pissed him off, but I don't care. This is my family, and I'll run it the way I see fit. The way my father would have.

"Now, if anyone else has a problem, they're welcome to stay home on Saturday," I say, looking at each man. "And make sure the soldiers are ready for a fight."

I'm not sure what's coming.

But my gut tells me it's bad.

LUNA

THE NEXT MORNING WHEN I WALK INTO THE KITCHEN, I
find my fiancé at the coffee machine. I didn't see him
last night, but I heard him come home. He didn't
venture into my bedroom, and I was thankful for it.
I needed the space.

"Good morning," I greet when I reach for a mug
which is just a little too high for me, and it causes
Enzo to grab it. He hands it to me, a gesture which
is both sweet, and shocking at the same time. It's not
like him to be nice to me. "Thank you."

He doesn't answer me. He doesn't even look my
way. Instead, he takes his mug and walks off to the
living room. Once he's settled on the sofa, I notice
him pull out his phone and tap the screen. Moments
later, two men walk in, one I recognize from the day

I arrived, and the other is new.

"I need you both to stay here today. There's something I need to check on, and I can't take her with me." His order has them nodding silently.

"I'm standing right here." I step into the space with the three foreboding men. It reminds me of being around my father when he has his soldiers and Capos around. When I was little, their presence used to scare me. But over time, I learned they were just normal men who had lives. Their wives and girlfriends loved them. Some even had children.

It was only their choice of job that made them scary.

But to me, they had become a sense of safety.

"I can see you're standing right there," he finally acknowledges my presence. "I wasn't talking to you. I was telling my men what their job is today."

"And what is *my* job? Cleaning the house? Doing the laundry?" I grit my teeth in frustration at the man I'm meant to marry. The man I should be obeying, and respecting, but when he treats me like a child, I'll act like one.

"Out," he orders the two guys who are standing at attention, their rapt gazes penetrating right through me. They're probably shocked at how I talked to their boss. Once they leave, Enzo pushes to his full height and towers over me. "Do you like to show off your sass in front of my men?"

"I just don't like being treated like I'm invisible." My voice quivers when he takes a step toward me. There are inches between us, and for once, I want him to lose control. I ache for him to do something, to kiss me. The realization doesn't shock me. I've wanted him since the night at Club Desperation. His handsome looks, his domineering persona, and his confidence captured my attention first. But seeing the pain in his eyes, after the mere mention of his family, makes him seem almost human.

"You're certainly not invisible, not to my men," he informs me. His words drag me from my thoughts, and my brows furrow. "Not when you're dressed like that." His sneer at my clothing hits me right in the chest.

The shorts are something I would normally wear to the mall, they're not overtly sexy. My loose-fitting top is see-through, sure, but underneath I have a strap tank top.

"There is nothing wrong with my clothes, most woman in the world dress the same way I do. It's hot in the apartment, and I'm not going to wear my winter clothes if it's so warm."

Enzo's glare only seems to intensify when he closes the last inch between us and grips my hips in his big, strong hands. His fingers dig into my curves, forcing a whimper to escape my lips.

The corner of his mouth tips upward at the

sound. "You're mine. My fiancée, so if other men, even my own fucking soldiers are looking at you as if you're theirs to fuck, then I have a problem with your outfit."

I won't let him dictate the way I live my life, certainly not what I choose to wear. "If you think I'm yours, then treat me the way I deserve to be treated," I throw back easily, my confidence a flickering flame in the storm that is Enzo de Rossi. For a long moment, we stand in silence, he doesn't release me, and I don't push him away. My head is tipped back, so I can look into those dark eyes. I don't know what I'm looking for, perhaps some form of affection. But all I find is flaming desire. "Then treat me like a woman, a partner."

"A partner?" He laughs darkly. "That will be a position earned. And if you want me to treat you like a woman, you'll be in pain for weeks after." His words hold a sexual vow that has my core clenching. "Do you want that, little dancer?" he taunts while tipping his head to the side as he regards me through black lashes. "You like the danger." It's not a question, so I don't answer.

His mouth is a sinister curve, reminding me of all the ways that Enzo de Rossi is bad for me. He may not love me, or I him, but there's an innate connection between us. A chemistry I've never felt with anyone before.

"Tell me, Luna," he says, his voice wrapping around my name like a lover, like a man who wants to own it. "Do you like it when I make you cry? Does your pretty pussy get wet when my blade trails its way down your neck, to your tits?"

"Enzo—"

"Do you touch yourself at night thinking about a man in the darkness taking you and making you come over and over on his cock?" His teasing tone has my clit throbbing, my pussy pulsing wildly with need.

"Enzo, please—"

My heart kicks against my ribs when his lips brush along mine. Heat courses through my veins, reminding me that I'm toying with a killer. His tongue darts out, tasting me ever so lightly. He doesn't make a move to kiss me, he doesn't pull me closer, even though I'm practically leaning into his broad frame.

"Do you want that man to be me, Luna? My little dancer," he coos, his voice silky soft, yet violently dangerous. The contrast causing the desire my belly to knot and tighten at the thought of him taking me. The idea of him stealing the one thing I still have that's mine to give. Only, Enzo doesn't know that, and I'm not telling him, not until that last minute.

His fingertips dig deeper, forcing another gasp from my lips, and suddenly, he swallows it with his mouth. He crashes into me, as if the clouds have come together and the rain can no longer hold off. His tongue dances along mine. He tastes of coffee, rich and chocolaty. The bitterness is how I imagined him to taste.

My body molds to his in a way that makes it feel as if I was made to fit with him. Two shattered fragments of the same whole. Enzo's hands trail from my hips to my ass, and he grips me harshly. Every sound I make, he inhales, as if he needs it to survive.

And as we fit together perfectly, I allow myself to wonder what it would be like if he did love me. His hands squeeze me harder, causing me to moan into his mouth. His lips are soft, but firm. Passion is this man's cologne, and he wears it like a fucking expert.

But then he pulls away. It's sudden, and I stumble backward. My body still buzzing with heat and desire still coursing through me when he stands before me, looking shocked. As if he didn't just willingly kiss me.

Seconds pass before he speaks again. "I'm meeting with my men. I'll be back in a couple of hours to pick you up." He spins on his heel and leaves me alone in the living room, my panties soaked, and my nipples hard like little pebbles against the tight fabric of my bra.

My mind is still dancing with the memory of his warmth. For a man so cold, so harsh, he's like a furnace, and I'm afraid he's going to burn me down.

For a long while, I stand there, looking at the door he walked through, wondering if he's finally breaking down the barriers he's built up. When I finally move, I head down the hall toward the bedrooms. Pausing at the door to mine, I glance over at Enzo's bedroom and make a beeline for it. The last time I was in here was my first day at the apartment, but now, as I step inside, it feels different. As if I'm meant to be here, rather than the guest room he's given me.

Everything has been tidied away. It's like he's not been here. I move into the bathroom where his scent is heaviest. The spice of his cologne has me inhaling deeply, and the memory of his kiss assaults me. When I open my eyes, I glance down to the corner of the room and notice the collar of one of his crisp white shirts. The splatter on the material is unmistakable—it's blood.

I pad over to it, picking it up to find the cuffs and forearms are stained in deep red. This is the life I'll live, where my husband comes home in someone's blood. Someone he's tortured, maimed, and killed.

I drop the item back in the laundry basket and pick up the whole thing before heading to the laundry room just behind the kitchen. I make quick work in getting everything on and as soon as the swish of water spins around the metal tub, I smile. Hopefully the stains will come out, and I hope that when Enzo returns, he'll be thankful for this, rather than admonish me.

In this moment, I feel confident I can do this.

I can be his wife.

I'm sure I can.

ENZO

Her taste is on me as I make my way into the office. The door clicks shut behind me, and I lock it. This needs to be private. Mario is already seated, waiting for me when I step inside. He glances over at me, arching a brow when I settle behind my desk. I'm five minutes late because of Luna. Because I let go of the control and restraint I'd been holding onto.

"I want to keep an eye on Valentino," I tell him without greeting. "Something is amiss at how he's against me taking over. I don't like it. The men should be behind me, not against me."

My best friend stares at me for a long while before he nods. "I can get that done. Care to tell me why you look so frazzled?" He leans back in his chair, his ankle resting on the opposite knee as he regards me with a smirk.

I shake my head. "No."

"Did something happen?" he continues to push, knowing he'll get something out of me if he keeps it up. Ignoring him, I open my laptop lid and turn it on. Mario sighs. "We've been best friends for years. I've known you since you were a kid. You cannot lie to me, even if you try," he informs me.

I open my email. I respond to two before I stop and look at him. Amusement dances in his eyes, he knows exactly what the reason is for me being distracted. "What we should be focusing on is getting information on the rest of the Cavallone clan that haven't been killed yet." I push to my feet and head to the safe which is hidden behind a painting my mother gave me on my twenty-first birthday. The waves crashing on the shore depicts a storm coming in the distance. Whoever painted it spent time at Black Hollow.

A small island of solace and calm.

The school is enormous, taking up half the island. The rest of it is owned by us and the Venier family. Since we no longer live in Italy, they run the school, along with the rest of the island.

"I'm just checking on you," Mario informs me. "You seem to be distracted. And the only person you saw and had intimate contact with before you walked into this office would have been Luna."

His smile is infectious, and for a moment, I allow myself to recall the kiss, how she tasted. The sounds she made had me hard as fucking rock, but then I realized what I was doing, letting her in. If I do that with her, she'll learn more about me, which means she'll be able to hurt me. I don't allow anyone to see the human side of me because it shows weakness.

As much as I want to sit down and figure out why I'm so enamored with her, beside the fact that she's not afraid of me, I can't. We need to be focused on the family, on how my father's legacy could come crashing down around me if I don't do something about it. We need to find the mole. And when we do, I'll end him. But I look at Mario before informing him of one simple truth, "she and I are a business transaction."

"Do all business transactions make you forget that today is my birthday?" Mario challenges, and I curse under my breath. I remembered when I woke up, and then Luna happened. It seems to be something I'm going to have to put up with for a long time to come — *Luna happened*.

"Fuck," I bite out. "Happy birthday, *amico*," I tell him. "My mind is on everything other than happy shit right now. We will party tonight." I go to him, my hand gripping his shoulder and giving it a squeeze of solidarity. "I'm sorry." I don't apologize to anyone, but he is like my brother, and I fucked up.

145

"Don't worry about it. I like to see you all over the place because of a pretty girl. Most women you've had don't even make you flinch. She, however, ..." He allows his words to taper off into the silence between us. "There's something about her that gets to you."

"We don't have time for this," I grit out in frustration when he hits the nail on the head. I take out the paperwork my father left behind for me in his safe and set it in front of Mario. "Read through this letter," I tell him, before settling back in my chair.

I wait in silence for him to finish, and when he does, his gaze lifts to mine with shock painting his expression. "So, this means your father didn't trust him either?"

Son, be wary of the snake that lies close to me. He will attack when the time is right. And I fear it is when you will rule.

The warning against my father's advisor is clear in his confession, written in ink, never to be doubted. "That is what's been bothering me. Why would my father tell me to watch the people closest to him? Not me, not us, but him." I pull up my email again, hoping I'll have an email from my father's lawyer about the reading of the will, but there's nothing. "I haven't heard from Romano yet," I tell Mario, concern niggling at me once more.

Mario's concern is etched on his face. We have both known the old man all our lives. He came here along with my father, and they were very close, closer than Dad was with Valentino, which makes me nervous. "Do you think something's happened?"

I pick up my phone, hitting dial on his number before I answer Mario. Pressing the device to my ear, I settle back and glance at Mario. "He's not answering." I'm on my feet in seconds, with Mario hot on my heels as we make our way down the hall to the elevator.

In the car, I'm tense. It's not a long drive to Romano's office, but gut instinct tells me what we're about to find isn't going to be pretty. By the time we pull up to the offices, I'm pushing open the door before the engine dies. Racing up the steps and through the front door, ignoring everyone around me. Mario is close behind me. In the elevator, we stare straight ahead in silence. The ride up to the top floor is anxiety-ridden, and I'm about to lose my control when the doors slide open.

When I reach Romano's office, I step over the threshold to the stench of death. "Fuck," the curse falls from my mouth unbidden. There, behind his ornate wooden desk, in his expensive office chair is Luigi Romano. In his hand is an envelope, his grip on it tight as his corpse cools. I'm across the room in

147

seconds. Touching his neck, I find nothing but ice-cold flesh.

He's been shot right through the head between the eyes. His lids are shut, and it looks like he's sleeping. But the hold he has on the document gives me pause. I pry it from his fingers, and find my name scrawled on the front. A wave of nausea hits me as recall my father's body. This was staged.

"What's wrong?" Mario asks, dragging me from the dark thoughts in my mind.

I glance over my shoulder at my friend. "This was done on purpose, for a reason. To send me a message." My voice is husky, rage has taken hold of me, and I'm ready to torture this bastard for what he's done. I have a feeling it has something to do with the will. It doesn't make sense, no matter who reads it, nothing will change. I still take over from my father. "Valentino did this."

He steps forward, stopping beside me. "How do you know?"

I turn to face Mario. "Because he was the only other man in the room when I found my father's dead body. Dad was holding a note that confessed he'd done something. The posed position, the way the eyes were closed, everything about it was exactly like this." I gesture with my hand toward Romano.

"Then it's time we take Valentino to the warehouse," Mario says what I'm thinking. The warehouse has always been for criminals who tried to hurt the family. For those who went against us, who tried to hurt us in some way, but this time, it's for one of our own. And I don't think he'll make it out alive.

I nod slowly, before I deliver my order, "Call the capos, I want them all there."

LUNA

I HAVEN'T SEEN HIM SINCE OUR KISS, AND MY GUT instinct is that he's hiding from me. Not because he's afraid, but because he's angry. He doesn't want to want me. The same way I don't want to feel anything for him, but the small glimpses of a man underneath the Boss I've seen have me intrigued.

I should be dancing or studying, but all I can focus on is how his body felt against mine and how his hands gripped me as if he was finally laying claim to me. The other thing that's been bothering me is our upcoming nuptials. He hasn't mentioned it again, and I haven't brought it up from fear he'll throw me out. I have nowhere to go, and I doubt Tommaso is going to welcome me back. He got rid of me the first chance he could.

I'm not his responsibility, which means I am more of a hinderance than anything else. Now that he's got my father's seat, the last thing he wants is his niece running around the house. When I hear the lock of the front door click, my heart rate spikes, and I'm pushing to my feet and rushing to the door before I know what I'm going to say.

But when I hear more than one set of footsteps, my heart plummets to my stomach. When I reach the living room, I find Enzo and Mario drenched in crimson. Both men have white shirts on that are now the color of red wine.

"What happened?" A gasp falls free from my mouth before I have time to think. Fear skitters down my spine like ice water freezing me in my advance.

Enzo glances at me from over his shoulder, his eyes manic with anger. "Go to your bedroom," he orders in a gruff tone, but I'm done being shoved around by men in my life.

"I'm not going anywhere until you tell me what the fuck happened," I grit, crossing my arms in front of my chest as frustration takes a hold of me.

Ever so slowly, Enzo turns on his heel and rounds the sofa. He reminds me of a lion about to chase the gazelle through the forest. He's so much taller than me, so much bigger. It's only when he's fully facing me that I get the full effect of the man, the monster, the Mafia Boss. Blood has stained his hands, his jaw, and with those dark eyes trained on me, for the first time in a long while, pure fear grips me.

"What did you say?" His words are controlled. A low gravelly threat drips from each syllable, his voice dark with danger and his face taut with annoyance.

"I... I-I just wanted to know what happened," I find my words, forcing my tone not to quiver when he stops inches from me. "W-why are you drenched in blood?"

Enzo silently lifts his hand, his thumb and forefinger grip my chin, and he tips my head so my eyes lock on his easily. So close, I can see the war raging within his stare, desire and anger, lust and pain, everything swirls within this man, and he never allows himself to let go.

Until the moment he kissed me.

The thought comes unbidden. It's the truth. And that's when I realize he doesn't hate me at all. He's angry that he wants me. The same way I'm frustrated that I want him.

"Are you worried about me, little dancer?" he coos against my lips, the metallic stench invading my nostrils.

"I-I..." I can't respond because his tongue darts out, sending an explosion of desire coursing through me as he gently licks at my mouth. He doesn't move closer. He doesn't kiss me. And I'm all too aware that Mario is watching our encounter.

"Did you think I was hurt? Were you going to kiss it better?" he whispers, each word feathering heat over my face, over my skin, causing goose bumps to rise in the wake of his taunts.

"Don't be an asshole," I bite out, swallowing past the lump in my throat. "I just..."

"You just?" he urges, tipping his head to the side as both his palms land on the wall either side of my head. I'm caged in, locked in a standoff with a predator, and I've never been more turned on. No, that's a lie, the last time I felt this way was when he gripped my neck, when he toyed with me, trailing his knife over my skin.

"I was worried," I finally admit, shame warming my cheeks, and I'm certain they're bright red. There's nowhere left to run, nowhere left to hide. Enzo can read me like a book, every page, every sentence, he knows what I feel, how he affects me, and he is using it to his advantage.

And there's nothing I can do to stop him.

"See how sweet she is, Mario," he taunts, but doesn't look at his friend, his gaze still on me as it trails over my face. "She was worried about her fiancé." He utters the last word with a thick accent which reminds me of who he is and where he's come from.

Suddenly, he presses his lips to my cheek before moving them along to my ear. Enzo captures the lobe between his teeth and bites down until I can't stop the whimper from escaping my lips.

When he releases the flesh from his mouth, I feel the smile on his face as it curls against my cheek. "Do you want Mario to watch while I make you come?"

My eyes snap open, and that's when I realize his best friend is watching us intently. "Stop it, Enzo." Even though I try to sound confident, my voice cracks around his name, desire pooling between my thighs.

"Are you sure, little dancer?" he continues to tease, the tip of his tongue tasting me, licking a white-hot path down my neck, before he sucks the flesh hard, his teeth grazing the sensitive skin sending more goose bumps skittering over me.

"Enzo," I bite out, my tone more confident, his name a warning on my tongue, and for a long while, he stays silent, then a low, rumbling chuckle vibrates through his chest, causing my nipples to harden against the tight top I'm wearing.

Enzo pushes away from me. The wolfish grin still there making my heart skip a beat when I take in just how handsome he is. "Someone killed my father's lawyer," he tells me suddenly, shocking me because I didn't expect him to admit something about his job to me.

"What?" My mouth falls open and I follow Enzo to the living room where he and Mario settle on the sofas. Both men still dirty. Their expressions cast with vengeance, and I have a feeling this has to do with my uncle. "Do you think it was Tommaso?"

Mario's gaze snaps to Enzo's, while my fiancé looks away and realization hits me right in the chest. The silence is deafening, but they don't have to tell me what I already know—my uncle is dead.

"I don't need protecting," I tell Enzo, hoping he'll just give me the honesty I need. It's the least he could do now that I have nobody.

Tears burn my lashes. I fight them, I don't want him to see me cry. My strength has always been my saving grace. It's what my parents taught me, mostly my father since he had been there longer than mom. But it was the one thing I learned from an early age.

"You're the fiancée of a Boss," Mario interjects. "Of course you need protecting." He pauses for a long while before continuing. "You are about to become a De Rossi, and when that happens, you'll be a target for a lot of bad people."

"I've been a target for bad people all my life," I throw back easily. It's as if he's forgotten who I am. A mafia fucking princess. "My father was also a Boss, he knew this life better than anyone, so don't tell me what I am."

"Enough," Enzo's voice booms in the space,

filling it up with his presence, and both Mario and I seem to shrink away. Those dark eyes pin me to the spot where I'm trying not to shy away from the force of Enzo. "You are going to be my wife, whether we like it or not." There's no longer a smirk on those perfect lips. "And when my men are there to protect you, it's because I put them there. Yes, you may come from this life, but you are still a woman. My woman. Am I clear?"

"I didn't think you'd protect someone you hate so much," I throw out, deep down wanting him to refuse that he hates me. I want him to feel something other than hate, and anger for me.

My chest tightens when he doesn't respond immediately, and I'm certain he's about to tell me he is only doing this because of his dad. "There is a fine line, little dancer," he speaks. "A very fine line."

"What?" I spit. "Between love and hate?" I sing song the words.

But my heart leaps into my throat when he says, "Between hate and obsession. And you are a fucking distraction," he admits, before his gaze flicks to Mario and then back to me. "I don't like being distracted."

"Then send me away." Even as I say it, I know I'm lying to him. I wonder if he can see it. If he can read through my facade and see just how much I don't want to leave. It makes no sense. Perhaps it's because I'm alone now. No parents, no uncle. It's just me against this life, against this world.

The corner of Enzo's mouth tilts slightly. Just a small bit which nobody would notice if they didn't know him. But I do. Now I do. And then he gifts me an answer that has my body turning rigid with shock. "Your name is signed in blood alongside mine, little dancer. The only way you'll ever escape me is in death."

ENZO

Glancing at the clock, I watch the minutes tick by as the red numbers tell me it's almost three in the morning. Darkness grips the apartment in its hold, as I paw through the paperwork Romano had in his office. Mario and I emptied out what we thought was important. Now, I have to wade through information before this evening's festivities.

I've been in two minds, wanting to take Luna with me, to show her what my life entails since she's so adamant to be a part of it. But I also want to show her who I really am. She's only seen me at home, and I know being cooped up in this apartment may be making her crazy.

I push to my feet and stretch. My back clicking in all the right places before I sigh and make my way to the living room where I pour a drink and settle at the large grand piano I bought when I moved into this place. It was perfect for this corner of the room with a view of the sparkling city below.

Setting the glass on the stool beside me, I allow my fingers to stroke the keys gently. My mind drifts to Luna in her bedroom, how she would sound if I were to touch her just like this. The smooth skin under my fingertips flourishing with goose bumps and a soft shade of pink. It always happens when I'm near her.

Earlier when I admitted to wanting her, to keeping her as mine, I noticed how her pupils flared. Mario is convinced the girl is falling for me, but I'm so much older than her. I'm a monster compared to her angelic beauty.

Even though she has grown up as a mafia princess, she still comes across as almost innocent. I close my eyes and play. The gentle notes of a contemporary song by Zolita filters through the room. 'Holy' with only the piano certainly sounds different as I go through the lyrics in my mind, while my vision is filled with Luna dancing in the studio.

How I wish she would dance for me.

I breathe deeply, and the scent of apples fills my senses. A small smile twinges on my lips. But I don't acknowledge her yet. Instead, I keep playing until the song hits it's crescendo and I'm lost in the melody.

The moment I hit the last key, silence rings in my ears, and I feel Luna padding closer, until she's inches from me. The heat of her body cocoons my back, but she doesn't touch me. Deep down, I want her to reach out to me. I have found myself focused on hating her, on being angry with her, but right now, all I want is for her to look at me as if I were a good man.

Like she looks at me when I touch her.

"You play beautifully," she remarks from behind me, her voice a whisper as if she's afraid she'll anger me. I don't respond, instead, I reach for my glass and tip it back until I've swallowed every drop. Then, I turn on the bench to face her.

She's dressed in a small pair of cotton shorts and a strap tank top that does nothing to hide her tits and nipples. The small peaks make my cock throb against my slacks. I haven't even changed, not since I walked in. I have shed my shirt, but I'm still in the clothes that smell of death.

"You look pretty in the dark," I tell her easily. "Pour me a drink, little dancer," I order her before handing her my tumbler. Without debate, she takes the glass and heads to the cabinet. I watch how her ass sways when she walks, and how those lithe legs glide through my home.

When she returns, I take the glass and set it

behind me on the top of the piano before reaching for her hips. I tug her closer, between my spread legs, and look up at her face. There are small lines across it from the pillow, her hair is a mess of dark strands, and her lips are fat and pouty which has me imagining her wrapping them around my cock.

"Will you ever not hate me?" she asks after a long silence. Her words shock me. Yes, I'm angry, yes, her family are my mortal enemy, but she, she's nothing but an obsession.

I can't stop the smile that curls my lips. "I don't hate you," I admit. It's only in the dark I would ever say this, at least for the first ten years of our lives together. "Like I said earlier, there is a fine line, and I've come to the conclusion that you're detrimental to me."

This has her tipping her head to the side, confusion clear on her pretty face. She is exquisite. In this light, as it shimmers off her perfectly formed cheekbones, and her pouty lips, she reminds me of a porcelain doll.

"Why would I be? It's not like I could kill you." Her choice of words has me chuckling.

I trail my hands up her hips, and then, slowly down her ass until I reach her thighs. Every movement I make has her breath catching. She's only ever seen me angry, only ever experienced me when I wanted to make her cry, but right now, all I want is to see her come apart for me.

I've waited far too long for this. "Will you obey me?" I ask, ignoring her earlier question. I don't want to delve into emotions. It's not the time or the place. My mind is still awash with the images I saw today. I've spent my life working for my father, and I've seen my fair share of death, but something clicked inside me today.

Something changed.

Luna nods, but she doesn't speak. "Sit on the piano," I order, before I lift her onto the bench, and I watch as she tentatively settles her pert behind on the smooth, shiny top of the grand. "Now spread your legs."

Her mouth opens, and I wait for her to retort, but she doesn't. Slowly, shyly, she obeys me and soon, I'm met with the material that hides her core from my view. With my fingertips on her ankles, I trail my way up her legs. Each inch I feather my touch along sends a shudder through her.

When her head drops back and a moan of pleasure falls from her lips, I'm certain I'm about to lose my mind. I reach her knees and push them wider before I get to her inner thighs. Her smooth flesh is dotted in goose bumps as I tug at the hemline of her shorts.

Pushing the garment to the side, I find her bare. "No panties?" My brow arches in question and she silently shakes her head. "Naughty girl." I tease her seam with my index finger which earns me a dick-throbbing whimper. "You know," I say as I taunt her with slow circles on her clit. "A hate fuck is more exciting than an evening of making love."

Her fingers curl around the top of the piano as she tries to focus on my words. I dip a finger into her, but not too deep. Her hips rise to meet my ministrations, and her thighs tremble as her feet slide beside my thighs.

The scent of her is intoxicating. I haven't ever smelled a woman so delicious, so mouth-watering before. "Because…" I continue as I insert a second finger, still not deep enough to give her what she needs. "The moment my cock stretches you without warning, when your body is shuddering and trembling beneath mine." I smile when she mewls my name. "That's when you'll beg me to make you scream. And I will."

"Please, Enzo!" Luna cries out and my cock leaks in my briefs. I'm sure there's a wet spot in my slacks. "Please."

"You'll beg and plead for my dick," I tell her, ignoring her pleas. "And I'll wait, and wait," I say as I continue teasing her. "And then, when you can't speak, when your voice is so broken from begging, I'll fuck you so hard, your body will bow for me. Your tight little cunt will mold to me, and you will only ever want me."

I pinch her clit with the last two words I utter, and she does scream my name so loudly, I'm sure the whole fucking New York City just heard her. I don't stop though, I continue circling her hardened little nub until her thighs are shaking uncontrollably, and her knuckles have turned white as she grips the piano.

Her back curves beautifully, elegantly as she leans back.

My cock is so sensitive, each movement against my briefs takes me closer to the edge. Slowly, I slide my fingers from her tight entrance. Luna lifts her head, her eyes are glazed with pleasure as she watches me lick each digit, tasting her flavor which bursts on my tongue.

"Such a good little dancer." I smile when her mouth pops open in shock. "Next time, I'll have you up there with your pointe shoes and leotard on." I push to my feet and help her to stand on shaky legs. Before she can take a step, I scoop her up and walk down the hallway toward her bedroom.

Her delicate hands on my bare chest send sparks of need through me, but I don't do anything more than setting her on the mattress and pulling the comforter over her curled up frame. When I reach the door, I grip the handle, wondering to myself just how I'm walking away from her instead of fucking her senseless.

The moment I step over the threshold, her voice comes to me, as if floating on a summer breeze. "Thank you for not hating me." I shut the door without responding, because deep down, if I were to say anything, it would flay me open and expose my humanity.

She's gotten to me.

She's burrowing under my skin.

And I have no way of getting her out.

LUNA

I HAVEN'T SEEN ENZO SINCE HE PUT ME TO BED AND LEFT me in my bedroom. Forty-eight hours is a long time to spend on tenterhooks, wondering if what you did was right. Or if he liked seeing me sitting on his piano, writhing like that. The memory blooms with warmth on my cheeks, spreading down to my chest as I roll over and squeeze my thighs together.

It's morning, and the apartment is silent. I have another hour before my classes start, and I know if I don't get up now, I'll be late. Sighing as I push the blankets off, I swing my legs over the edge of the bed and glance at my nightstand to find a small black envelope.

The scrawl on the front is familiar—Enzo.

Opening it quickly, I pull out a little note which

has his handwriting over both sides of the page.

Work is busy. I don't owe you anything, not an explanation, but I find myself needing to leave this. My mind has been swamped with memories. I don't like it. I'm not a man who allows emotion into his world because it can be fatal, but you, little dancer, have pranced your way into my ordered life and sent it into a fucking whirlwind.

When I arrive home tonight, I expect you to be at the dining table waiting for me. There is no debate. You will wear black. Your hair will be loose, straightened down your back. And you will not be wearing any underwear. It is time I claimed my soon-to-be wife.

It's not signed.

I shove the small note back into its envelope and close it, setting it on the nightstand as I try to forget his words. The other night seems to have meant nothing because he doesn't want to allow me in. Emotion and I come hand in hand. I never once expected the man to love me, especially when he's been forced to marry me, but he doesn't even consider me a partner.

Taking his last name is the only thing that's left to do, but I have a feeling even though I will be addressed as a De Rossi, my blood will always be Cavallone. I quickly get ready for dance classes, and rush into the kitchen to grab some fruit and a coffee.

But the moment I step foot in my studio, I find Mario settled at a small table, his focus on a laptop and the music gently playing a rendition of 'Monster' by Meg Myers. He doesn't look up when I walk in.

"Hello," I greet, causing him to snap those silver eyes on me. "I'm sorry, I didn't mean to interrupt. It's just... I'm about to have a class." I make my way closer, hoping to not seem like an annoyance if he's working.

"I know." He nods before turning his attention back to the screen.

My brow furrows. "But you can't be in here."

"I can be wherever Boss wants me," he tells me without looking up which rattles me. *Boss*. Of course, Enzo has his best friend watching me.

"I can take care of myself, it's only a freaking dance class." My voice drips with frustration as I head to the stereo to turn it off. The room is suddenly filled with a heavy silence that makes me nervous.

He types away at his laptop, and I'm convinced he's ignoring me but when I turn to do my stretches, his voice echoes off the walls. "There are threats anywhere," Mario says. "I am here not only to watch you and ensure you're not killed, or maimed in any way, but to also be there for the man who's been my best friend all my life."

I glance at him from over my shoulder. "But I'm nothing to him. I'm a contract. If I were to be killed, he'd be free."

This time, Mario pushes to his full six-foot-five height and stalks toward me as if he's about to strangle me himself. "If you don't realize by now just how much Enzo cares for you, then you're either blind, stupid, or both." The frustration in his voice, etched on his face is clear. He is practically vibrating with rage, but he doesn't once touch me. I wonder briefly if it's an order that comes from above, if Enzo told him he's not allowed to lay a hand on me.

I tip my head back in defiance, my hands landing on my hips. "He has never once let me in. He has never once told me—"

"If you think Enzo de Rossi is going to proclaim his undying love for you, then you'll die before you hear it. The man has built up his walls so high, not many can scale them. But once you've burrowed yourself into his life, there's no going back."

"Are you trying to say your Boss has a crush on me?" I laugh out loud. The disbelief is clear in my tone. "Because all he's ever done is make me come on his fingers, and even then, he put me to bed, and I haven't seen him in two days."

Just then, the door to the studio slams against

the wall, sending a trickle of ice down my spine. He doesn't move. He doesn't speak. Mario straightens, his eyes focused above my head, which is easy since I'm so much shorter than him. But there's no mistaking who is at the door.

"Go down to the car and make sure it's ready," his order comes quickly, but still filled with the violence I've come to expect from Enzo. Mario moves without question, and soon, it's only me and my fiancé.

"Where is my teacher?" I ask as I turn to regard him. He's dressed in a pair of dark jeans which hug his muscled thighs. The button up he's wearing is a charcoal gray that seems to be painted onto his broad frame. I swallow past the lump in my throat when he looks at me as if he's about to devour me.

"You're coming with me today," he announces. "Put some sweats on, I'm not taking you out with nothing but those fucking tights.' His hungry glare drinks me in, eating me up from head to toe.

"But—"

"Did I give you an option?" he questions, his teeth clenching with frustration, his jaw ticking, and his hands fisting at his sides. I know if I push further, if I nudge just a little more, he'll lose control.

Do I want him to?

Yes. Of course.

But I have a feeling where we're going, it has

nothing to do with our relationship, or the unbidden desire between us.

"So, are you going to ignore what happened between us? Do you think the note you left was sufficient explanation?" I ask because my curiosity has been through the roof since that night. And finally having Enzo before me has me on edge. The look of disbelief on his face is clear. My retort has his expression painted with guilt and something I can't quite put my finger on—frustration perhaps.

His note didn't give away much of his thoughts, that he *did* feel the need to leave one. A man doesn't drop a note on the pillow if there aren't emotions involved. Surely. I am certain I wasn't the only one affected by our encounter. The thought makes me smile. Because I want to, no, I need to make him feel something.

"We're about to go to my warehouse," he answers. "You'll see me torture and possibly kill a man, perhaps once I'm through, we can talk about how your tight little pussy drenched my fingers."

For a moment, I'm confused as to why he's taking me with him, but I don't question it, instead, I nod. "Fine, I'll change." I rush into my bedroom and pull on a pair of sweatpants and a T-shirt. I slip into my sneakers and race back down to find Enzo in the kitchen.

He's swallowing back a shot of espresso when

I stop at the counter and stare at him. When those cocoa eyes land on me, he arches a dark eyebrow, and takes in my outfit.

"Ready?"

I nod slowly, still nervous, and unsure of why he's taking me with. "Yeah," is all I manage before we're out the door and heading to the garage. In the car, the silence hangs heavily, reminding me that this isn't some fun outing, we're going to a place that holds death in its grip.

Enzo doesn't speak, neither does Mario and it sets me on edge. My stomach twists, and my hands are sweaty. I swipe them down my thighs, but it doesn't help. I'm about to slide them under my legs when Enzo grabs one, his fingers wrap around mine, and he pulls my palm to his lap.

I'm shocked speechless, but the look on Mario's face screams, *I told you so.* And my cheeks heat as I realize he obviously knows his best friend far better than I know my fiancé. The only question that now hangs in the balance is, *have I managed to make the king fall?*

LUNA

Violence.

Destruction.

The fall of a man who wronged a mafia family.

As we walk into the warehouse, Mario behind me, and Enzo leading us, my stomach twists with anticipation, anxiety, and something akin to fear. The whispers I've eavesdropped on while growing up was enough to give me nightmares, but I never once witnessed what my father did to the men who disobeyed him.

The moment the rest of the men see me, silence hangs heavily in the enormous warehouse. I can *feel* their judgement as to why Enzo brought me here today. I want them to know I'm here because I am marrying their boss, but I stay silent, knowing my place by his side should be done in silence.

"Ciao," Enzo greets as he walks past each of the suits who stand with their spines straight and their jaws ticking with frustration at my presence. "My fiancée wanted to see the work I do," he says, causing me to snap my gaze toward him. This was his idea. *Bastard*. "She needs to learn how this life works and I trust you will respect her, as you do me."

"Si, of course. You know we will always respect your wishes; we are Familia," one of the men says. His dark hair is peppered with silver and his eyes have crow's feet at the edges. He regards me with charcoal gray eyes, the color of storm clouds as they descend, but he doesn't speak to me.

"What am I doing here, Enzo?" That's when I see the older man in the chair, bound, bleeding from his lip. Enzo doesn't respond, instead, he stalks closer to the chair, stopping inches from him.

"We need to have a talk, and I wanted the rest of the men here to witness what is about to happen," Enzo tells him, his tone icy, his hands fisting at his sides as he regards the chained man. "Now, tell me Valentino, have you heard what happened to Romano?" Enzo asks.

The man who I now recognize to be the one who stood by when my uncle brought me into the warehouse when I was first given to Enzo shakes his head slowly. But there's something about his demeanor that tells me he's lying. His tongue darts out to lick at the blood at the side of his mouth, but it's how his gaze flits back and forth at the rest of the room that confirms he's lying.

Enzo straightens to full height, towering over the man while sneering down at him. His face is a picture of pure rage. "Do you really think I'm going to believe a lying man?" he challenges Valentino, a sinister smile curling his lips. Enzo de Rossi is the epitome of a bomb just waiting to go off. Coiled like a serpent, seconds away from striking.

"You have no right to sit on your father's chair," Valentino spits, anger clear in his voice. "I don't know what you *think* you know," he says. "But I would watch my tongue if I were you, little boy."

Enzo moves so quickly, I almost miss it when I blink, the sharp steel of his weapon glittering in the yellow light that hangs overhead. His fingers curled tightly around the handle, and everything south of my belly button twists with the reminder of when he used it on me.

This time when he wields it though, there's violence in his stance, in his movements. The slick tip meets Valentino's chin. The sharpness of the metal pierces skin, and a small pearl of crimson forms on the silver. Stark contrasting colors remind me of who my future husband is.

"Tell me again what you think of me," Enzo urges as he slips the knife between the older man's lips. "Tell me how you think I'm nothing but a little boy," he murmurs, his tone turning dark, sending fear skittering down my spine. I've seen him angry, but this is beyond comprehension. "Also, tell me what happened to my father." The last few words are a mere whisper, but we hear it. All of us standing witness to what's about to happen, seem to hold our breaths as we watch the scene play out.

A croak of agony comes from the older man as blood drips over his lips. The dark red fluid soaking his pristine white shirt, but Enzo doesn't stop. He continues to press down on Valentino's tongue. Bile rises in my throat, and as if he can read my mind, Enzo pins me with a dark look.

"This is the man you're going to marry," he tells me, the husky gravel of his voice scraping itself over my skin causing goose bumps to erupt. "Will you want me after I'm soaked in Valentino's blood?"

A cry of agony escapes his victim, and Enzo smiles. "You're a fucking monster, your father would never—" At the mention of his father, Enzo's blade slides through Valentino's shoulder like a warm knife through butter. Screams and curses erupt from the older man as my fiancé's hand is stained in the life force he's drawing from his victim.

I thought I would be scared, but as I swallow

back my fear, and the acid sitting in my throat, I realize something else, that Enzo isn't a monster at all. He's doing this because he believes this man has murdered Romano, who I now guess is the lawyer.

"Enzo," I call to him, hoping he'll look at me so I can show him I'm not afraid of him. When those dark eyes pierce me, I say, "I am yours. And I'm not scared." My words slowly reach him as I whisper them, and I notice the change in his expression when he realizes what I've just admitted.

I can't say I love him. Not yet anyway.

But deep down, there's something innate between us, we're tethered, connected and I want him to know that I'm not running away. I came into this wanting to break him, but I have a feeling he'll be the one breaking me.

"You," Valentino suddenly spurts, his glare on me. "It's your fucking family who broke us," he says, his voice demonic as his rage consumes him. "You want someone to blame," he mutters, through clenched teeth before looking back at Enzo. "Blame her godforsaken uncle."

"What?" Both Enzo and I say the word at the same time, shock clear in both our voices as we wait for an explanation. I'm about to step forward, but Mario grips my arm, holding me back. When I glance over my shoulder, he shakes his head.

"Her uncle isn't dead." Valentino chuckles.

"He's waiting, building his army from the ground up, and when he comes for the De Rossi clan, you'll all be dead, including the whore." That's when I see fury take over Enzo, I see the beast hidden beneath his perfectly formed veneer. His shiny suits, his crisp linen shirts hide the person that grips the older man's face, and he slices at each corner of the wrinkled mouth.

Agonizing wails bounce off the metal walls, echoing around us, a symphony of violence and the stench of death is already hanging in the air. It permeates our clothes, our flesh. There's no doubt I'll be washing it off for weeks to come.

"This is what happens when you hurt a De Rossi, when you go against the Familia," Enzo murmurs before he shoves the blade down Valentino's throat, and I'm almost certain he's about to cut his tongue out, but he doesn't. The horrific scene before me gets worse when he slices the man's tongue in two. "A fucking snake," Enzo hisses with a grin that's pure rage.

The moment the sight comes into view is when my stomach turns, and I race for the door. I make it out just in time. I hurl once, twice, before I feel hands on me. I don't smell blood, so it can't be Enzo, which means its Mario.

"Are you okay?" His familiar voice questions gently. His touch is warm, calming almost, and for a moment, I focus on him rather than what I've just seen.

"Yes," I answer before I swipe the back of my hand over my mouth. A white handkerchief appears, and I take it happily, using it to wipe away any mess I made. When I straighten, I look up into Mario's eyes that are filled with concern. "I thought I could handle it." A sense of dread takes over me.

Can I really do this?

Can I be the wife of a man who can so easily maim another?

"It's never easy to see, but what you have to remember is that if Enzo doesn't make a spectacle, the men will think he's weak." There's a small smile on his face, and I know he means well. But I feel like the weak one. I should know Enzo has to do this as he takes his father's seat at the table.

"It's still strange for me to watch," I tell Mario. "I knew my father did things like that all his life, but actually witnessing it..." I shake my head as I allow my words to filter into the silence which fills the space between us.

"Let's go," Enzo says suddenly, shocking me back to life. He's got his phone in hand as he makes his way to the car, while the rest of the men file out of the warehouse. "Get the clean-up crew at the warehouse now. I don't give a shit what you do with the body."

The moment I slip into the backseat of the SUV, Enzo's hands are on my hips, tugging me over his lap, causing a squeak of surprise to fall from my lips. He smells of violence and death, but seconds before I can question what he's doing, his mouth slams down on mine.

His tongue darts alongside mine, the warmth of him, mingled with the memory of what he's just done has me reeling as I twine my hands behind his neck. But that's when I remember I puked, and I pull away, needing space.

"I...I puked," I whimper when his fingers dig into my hips.

The corner of his mouth tilts, as if he's already considered that. "You're my fiancée, I'll kiss you any fucking time I want." His voice is husky sending shivers down my spine. "I want nothing more than to take you home and fuck you," he says, the admission causing my thighs to clench around him. And he grins, knowing his filthy mouth is making me needy.

"I'm sorry I ran out," I tell him.

"Oh, my little dancer, that was only the first of many times you'll be by my side when I'm on a job. I like getting my hands dirty," he informs me, the wolfish grin filled with amusement is back on his face now. The earlier anger gone. "You'll get used to it."

"Why take me with anyway?"

"I want you to know me," Enzo admits soberly. "Because when you say those two little words on our wedding day, I need you to know exactly who you're marrying."

As his words sink in, I lean against his chest, wondering if this is the first sign of him feeling something for me. It must be.

I'm knocking the king from his perch.

Now, I just need to make sure I don't fall as well.

ENZO

Settling Luna in her bed, I stand watch over her for a long while after she's fallen asleep. I carried her from the car, all the way to the apartment, and then, set her on the soft mattress. What happened in the car, the kiss, how beautifully she moaned into my mouth, even as I held her drenched in another man's blood, it flicked a switch inside me.

I promised her a day of normality outside the apartment. Instead, I took her to watch me cut a man's tongue in two. Mario and Thiago have gone to search Valentino's apartment for info. I'm certain there'll be skeletons hidden in his closet.

Luna rolls over, her moan loud enough for me to hear, and loud enough for my cock to take notice. I don't know how long I stand at her bedside, but when her lashes flutter and she opens her eyes, a gasp of surprise tumbles from her plump lips.

"What are you doing?" Luna questions as she scoots up against the headboard. Her eyes are wide now, and I can tell she's tired from the way they're slightly sleepy as she attempts to focus on me.

"I was just watching you," I tell her honestly. This strange relationship of ours hasn't started off in the best way. And though I still hate her father, and her uncle, there's something about Luna I cannot despise.

"You know that's considered creepy," she informs me, her lips pouting in frustration as she crosses her legs, and for a long moment, I'm hit with the fact that she's only eighteen, going on nineteen. She's so fucking young, and yet, most days, I forget.

"Consider me your creepy fiancé." I shrug as if it's nothing, but as the words free themselves from my mouth, it's the first time I feel as if I'm coming to terms with the fact that she's mine and I'm hers.

Luna stares at me for a long time before she smiles. "I didn't think I would be able to admit that to myself, let alone anyone else." Her youth shines through her words. The gentle light from the moon hanging outside her window, as if watchful that she's safe, illuminates her.

Angelic.

It's the only word I can use to describe her as

she sits on her bed, her knees now pulled up against her chest, and her arms wrapped around her legs. Luna rests her chin on her knees, as her wide eyes regard me.

"Have you ever felt lonely in this life?" she asks then, natural curiosity shimmering in her gaze and my chest tightens, twisting with something I can't quite put my finger on.

I consider her question for a long while. Mario has been my best friend, but even so, he's always had his own life. Growing up, I was alone a lot. With my father focused on the family, I was left to my own devices, which led me to the path I'm on now. And then I look at Luna and gift her the most honest response I can, "All the time."

"Me too." Her voice is a whisper, a pained murmur of admission. I didn't expect us to connect in any way. Since the moment I first saw her dancing on stage, to the moment I signed the fucking contract, I convinced myself Luna was a young, innocent girl who will only get in my way.

But looking at her now, I realize there's fragility in her strength, and heartache she's had to bear which matches my own. Not only growing up in a Mafia family, but losing parents, being alone in this world, and not being able to admit it to anyone.

My father taught me that telling anyone what you're feeling is a weakness. So, instead of admitting my pain, I buried it down deep, until there was nothing but a harsh, cold heartless man. That is what I am now. And I know it.

Luna deserves more.

She deserves better.

"I'm sorry my uncle killed your parents," she mumbles, her eyes downcast, her mouth twisted at the corners. "I know what it's like to find your father like that, and I wouldn't wish it on anyone," she tells me. "Not even my worst enemy." With that, she looks up and meets my inquisitive stare.

That's exactly what I am to her—an enemy.

"I don't blame you for wanting to escape this," I tell her. "I wanted out as well, but now that we're here, I think..." Shaking my head, I push to my feet. I can't do this with her, not right now. I'm still reeling from what Valentino said, my mind isn't clear enough to dig deep with Luna tonight.

I turn for the door, needing to make my escape.

"Do you always do that when things get tough?" she throws at my back before I reach her bedroom door. Her words have me stilling all movement.

"Do what?" I keep my voice even, calm, but my blood is warming with need to make her pay for something, for anything.

"Run away from feeling something." Every inch of my body tenses, before I slowly turn on my heel. When Luna notices my stance, she shifts on the bed before getting to her feet, and I realize she wants to run. I've always allowed anger to spark me first, and this time it's no different. I move swiftly, too quick for her.

The moment my hand grips onto her neck, a squeak leaves her lips and I want more sounds from her. Pinning her against the window, I smile when she shivers at the cold. Outside, the night air is icy, inside though, I'm boiling.

I reach for my blade and bring it up to her face. "I walk away when it's time to leave," I inform her before I trail the sharp steel along her top which falls away easily, bearing her tits to my hungry stare.

She shakes her head, fear dancing in her pretty eyes. "I-I didn't mean—"

The knife reaches her hips, and I slice away the sweats she's wearing. Soon, all my pretty little dancer is wearing, is a pair of tiny black lace panties. I step away, releasing her and she almost falls to her knees.

God, what a sight that would be.

"Dance for me," I tell her as I settle in the wingback chair that I had put in here at the window so she could sit and read. My legs are spread, and I'm twirling the knife at my knee, the glint dancing along the walls in the dim light.

Her mouth pops open in shock, her hands fisting at her sides, but thankfully she doesn't try to hide her beautiful curves from my view. "What?"

"You heard me," I say, gesturing with my chin. "Dance for me."

Luna tips her chin upward, defiance clear in her features as she shrugs nonchalantly, but I can see her hands trembling. She flicks the stereo on and a song filters through the speakers which I've set up in each corner of her room.

The melody takes hold of her, and she moves elegantly. Her hips sway, her hands trail up and down her curves as she twists and turns on the lush carpet. She closes her eyes, not looking at me, but I know she can *feel* my stare on her. She moves with the grace of a princess, but when she dips her hands down to her toes, my cock, and my mind jolt with want.

Her panties have a wet spot forming between her thighs. I can see it from where I'm seated. Her ass fat and round, making my dick throb against my zipper. Lithe legs spread, until all I can see, is her. "Come here," I order. When she rises and turns to me, I smile, but it's not friendly, it's depraved. "Crawl to me."

Her mouth opens, but I lift a finger to my lips to silence her. For a long while, my defiant little dancer glares at me, but then she obeys, and I grin. When she reaches me, she stops, sitting back on her heels as she regards me from the floor.

"Take my cock out," I order, my voice gravel with desire. Her dainty fingers fiddle with my zipper, and when her hand wraps around my cock, I almost lose it. My control slips when she strokes me, once, twice, before I grab her wrist to stop her.

I lift the blade I'd been holding with my other hand, and I flick it around so I'm holding the sharp end. The handle is a smooth leather which I taunt her lips with, and the little minx shocks me speechless when she wraps those plump lips around it and sucks it into her mouth.

Her eyes blaze with defiance and hunger. I pull the weapon from her lips and wait, but I don't have to wait long because Luna's mouth is on my dick within seconds, and I almost come in her mouth before I have time to think things through.

"Fuck," I curse, the word is grit through my teeth as pleasure zings through my body. It's as if taking a shot right to the vein. She slides down my dick, all the way until I'm hitting the back of her throat, the soft choking sound making my balls draw up. Tangling my free hand in her hair, I pull her from my cock with a wet pop. "Up."

Luna stumbles to her feet, her knees wobbly as I lead her to the bed, pushing her down on her back and sliding my blade under the soft material of her panties. The moment they fall free from her body, I'm met with the sight that's kept me awake for months.

"Spread your legs, little dancer, let me see what I own." She silently obeys. Her body shudders as she watches me with wide eyes. I drop to my knees like a sinner in church and mark a path from her ankle to her inner thigh with my knife.

When I reach the soft flesh just inches from her pussy, I push the blade deeper, making sure to remind her who she belongs to. The crimson droplet that escapes has my dick throbbing wildly. I lean in without saying a word, and lap at the metallic fluid, savoring her life force on my tongue.

A whimper escapes Luna's lips, her hands tangling in my hair, attempting to pull me closer, to where she needs me, but with another flick of my wrist, another droplet appears on her other thigh. A warning. And she releases me.

"Please, Enzo," she pleads, her eyes wide, glassy as she looks down at me between her perfect thighs. I lap at her blood, enjoying the tang as it hits my taste buds. I continue taunting her with a pinch here, and a pierce there, and soon, her hips are rising and falling, her cunt drenched as her juices drip down her ass.

"Beg me for more," I growl, my mouth inches from her core. The scent of her arousal sending me reeling over an edge I never want to come back from. I drop the knife to the floor, before I suckle on the wound I made on her smooth, porcelain skin. It's tiny, but the more I suck on it, I know it hurts.

My teeth graze her flesh, causing her thighs to quiver. I bite down hard, earning myself a scream of unadulterated pleasure. When my mouth pops off her leg, I bask in the beautiful red circle left behind.

"Every time you close your legs tomorrow, and days from now, it will be the memory of me on your mind," I promise her, before doing the same thing on her other leg.

Luna meets my gaze then. Her face the picture of seduction and innocence, a contrast if ever I saw one. And she says the words I've been dying for her to say since the moment I first laid eyes on her, "Enzo, please just fuck me."

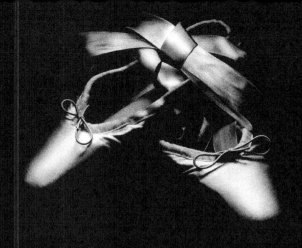

LUNA

It's as if something inside him snaps. My words, the chemistry that sizzles between us, has Enzo gripping my ankles, and tugging me down the bed until my ass hits the edge. He nestles himself between my thighs.

"You've wanted my cock since you first saw me," he taunts, making my cheeks heat. "Didn't you, little dancer?" He doesn't bother taking off his clothes, he grips his shaft which is hard from moments ago when I had him in my mouth, and he strokes himself.

The hypnotic movement makes my core clench, knowing what he's about to find out. He's going to know what I've been hiding from him. He drops one hand to the mattress which lands beside my head.

The other, positions himself at my entrance.

"Last chance to back out," he murmurs along my lips, but the bastard knows I'm not going anywhere. I told him at the warehouse that I'm here to stay.

I offer him a smile. "Do it," I challenge, urging him by wrapping my legs around his waist. The small incisions he made with his blade sting when my flesh meets the material of his slacks.

Enzo notices the wince on my face before he nudges the tip of his weeping cock against my pussy. "Fuck," he curses under his breath when he pushes inside.

"Do it, Enzo, show me what a monster you are," I mumble against his mouth, my tongue darts out to lick at his lips and it releases the feral beast within because in one brutal thrust, he's fully seated inside me.

Pain explodes through every nerve-ending in my body, reminding me that my future husband now owns every part of me. Even the most valuable of all. Enzo stills, his body tense as my nails dig into his shoulders through the material of his shirt.

"Luna," he whispers in a tone that is a stark contrast to the violence he just slammed into me with. "Luna," he says my name again, and I finally open my eyes, allowing him to see the truth swimming in the tears that have collected on my lashes. "You were a virgin."

Slowly, silently, I nod.

"Jesus," Enzo grits through clenched teeth. He's so tense, he doesn't move. The thickness of him fills me to the brim, and I'm sure he's going to split me in two the moment he does slide out and in, the moment he fucks me, I'll break, and I realize I've made the king fall, but I'm tumbling alongside him into the abyss. "Why didn't you tell me?"

My throat works past the lump that's formed, and I stare into those dark orbs. "Because I didn't need you to look at me differently," I tell him in a broken whisper. Reaching for his face, I cup my hands on his cheeks before I murmur, "I wanted your darkness."

And that's when he moves. His hips sliding back, sending more pain coursing through me, and then, Enzo slams back in. My pussy is wet, but it feels as if he's tearing through me. A storm waging war on the land beneath it. And I'm sure there'll only be destruction in its wake.

He slides out, and thrusts two more times before he stills when he's so deep inside me, I'm convinced he's hitting my stomach from the inside.

"Luna, I..." Enzo shakes his head, his focus blurring as my tears falls freely now. The pain, the tension. "Let go, stop tensing like that." He reaches for my face, gently stroking my cheek before he drops his hand between us and circles my clit with his thumb. The sensation of pain mingled with pleasure sparks in my brain like fireworks going off.

"Enzo," I call out his name, my back arching off the bed when he captures a nipple in his mouth and suckles on it while he teases my bundle of nerves with his expert touch. My thighs shake as pleasure takes over the pain, and Enzo starts moving slowly this time. He pulls out almost all the way, and gently, ever so torturously, slides inside me, his cock throbbing as it fills me, and I'm not sure where the fine line between pleasure begins and pain ends.

They live together harmoniously as he fucks me.

His mouth, his hands, his body worships mine like a sinner praising the darkness. Enzo makes my body pulse and drip, and when he moves faster, I meet him thrust for thrust. My hips lifting as he slams me into the mattress. The gentleness long gone, and in its place, is the hungry desire that's hung between us for weeks.

"Come for me, little dancer," Enzo coos against my cheek, capturing my mouth as a cry of pleasure is ripped from my core when his fingers pinch my clit and his cock seats deeply inside me.

"Oh god," I cry out as an orgasm strangles me and twists low in my belly. My pussy pulses around Enzo's cock and that's when I feel his hips jolt and warmth floods me on a low groan from the man who has just taken my virginity.

We lay in sweaty silence for a long time. When Enzo's cock finally slips from me, I wince at the emptiness I feel. He doesn't say a word as he pushes to his feet and leaves me for a moment to fetch a cloth from the en suite. He cleans me up, and I notice the blood on my inner thighs and on his cock.

He grips the shaft, his hand stained with my innocence, and he strokes it slowly. I snap my questioning gaze to his. The corner of his mouth tilts upward in a wolfish grin. "I love being coated in your blood, little dancer, but this," he says, lifting his hand to his nose, inhaling my essence. I want to crinkle my nose at the motion, but also, can't deny it is the hottest thing I've ever seen. "It's like heroin. A shot straight to my vein."

My cheeks burn with embarrassment as I take in the man before me, tall, rugged, still in his clothes, bar for his cock that's now softening. He turns and leaves me once more, and when he returns, he's shirtless.

It's the first time I've seen him look so beautifully erotic. The way his slacks hang low on his hips, the smooth, tanned skin of his torso tensing and releasing with every step.

"I don't sleep with women," he tells me. "But I'll make an exception tonight." He slips into the bed beside me and pulls me closer. I'm thankful he didn't leave me in here alone, not tonight of all nights. "Sleep now, little dancer."

"Are you happy you were my first?" I ask, my back cocooned to his front so I can't see his eyes, I can't see his expression when I voice my question. But the way his arm tenses around me tells me that his possessive nature has now taken hold.

"I told you you're mine," he whispers in my ear. "And it didn't matter if I got your virginity or not, but yes." A smile on his lips curves across my cheek. "I'm a caveman, and if you weren't in my house right now, I would've dragged you by your hair and locked you up right here."

"I think I'd like that," I mumble as the image of him acting like a crazy person just for me lingers in my exhausted mind. It's been a long day, but right now, I'm safe. I haven't felt like this in... forever.

"Perhaps one day we'll play that game," Enzo says gently. "Sleep now." The order comes swiftly, but softly, and I nuzzle myself into his arms and allow my lashes to flutter closed. I just pray that when I wake, this wasn't all just a dream.

ENZO

Nothing comes close to what I'm feeling.

When I woke this morning at three, the usual time my body reacts to a new day, I slipped from Luna's bed, leaving her curled in the blankets. It's the first time I've ever spent more than a few moments in bed with a woman while she slept.

It's not something I do.

But after I took her purity like a savage, I couldn't bring myself to walk out. As much as I needed space to think, I held her, wrapping her in my arms, and for the first time since we met, she didn't fight me.

Toying with her last night, tasting her blood was exhilarating. She wasn't afraid of me, but rather edged me on, urging me to show her my demons. There are so many things I'd like to do with her,

197

which I haven't done with anyone before. Not because I couldn't, but because I didn't trust myself with anyone else.

With her, I feel more at ease than I imagined. Even though she's so much younger, she challenges me like no woman can or has done. I can tell she enjoys the rough handling I love to dole out, and I have a plan to make sure we both bask in the darkness.

My office door opens, Mario and Thiago step inside, and I realize I need to focus on work rather than my pretty little dancer. My men settle in the seats, their stoic expressions are clear giveaways that they've found evidence we wanted against Valentino.

"I didn't want this to be the answer," Mario tells me as he sets a stack of photographs, along with documents on my desk. My stomach twists with anxiety when I pick up the first few photos. Someone has been following me, and watching Luna. The pictures of her are from before she came into my care, but there is no mistaking, whoever it is has gotten close to her.

Too close for fucking comfort.

The rest of the images are of myself with Mario, with a few of the other men in our family. They know our haunts. Of course, Valentino would've known all of this before, but it's what's in the documents that follow which is cause for concern.

Emails back and forth between him and Tommaso dated only days ago. A clear indication that he didn't in fact kill Luna's uncle, instead, he was working with him to bring down the De Rossi family.

"Who was there after we left?" I ask, poring over the emails, scanning them for names, for information I can use to eradicate the moles and snakes from my family.

"There were a couple of the soldiers, but nobody else was witness to what went down," Mario tells me, his voice is filled with the same violent rage that I currently have coursing through my veins.

"I want them all in here," I tell him. "Bring each and every man to my office because I want to know what they saw. I don't care if they were outside at the time." My order is clear. The rat has been found, but I have a feeling that someone else was helping Valentino. "And while you're at it, I want each of the capos brought in. One by one."

Mario nods. Thiago looks at me, wariness on his features. "I have connections with a few of the FBI who have been sniffing around," he tells me. "I can see if they know anything about the Cavallone family."

"That's a good idea. If you can reach out to them, and with me questioning my men, we can get to the bottom of this. I don't want gossip to be spread, so let's keep this under wraps until I've figured out the next step."

"I'm sure once you start questioning the men, they'll get talking." Mario's right. I can't risk having them whispering about what we're doing.

"A party," I say suddenly when it comes to me.

Mario's brows furrow in confusion at my detour. "What?"

"I'll have a party at the house before we go to the harbor," I announce. It's been three years since I walked into that building. More so because I found my parents slain in my father's office. But also, because there are ghosts that have lingered from before I was born.

"You mean the De Rossi mansion?" Mario's question is filled with shock. I nod. "Well, that is certainly a different path."

"I need to go there at some point. I guess I can't hide from my past forever." I'm not sure why I'm ready to go there now, but having a party, while bringing each man into my father's office, where he was murdered would break them. They've been loyal to the De Rossi family for years, and to stand in the room where their Boss was murdered, may shake them up.

"Does this have anything to do with your new wife?" Thiago asks, a smirk sliding over his face as he regards me. We all grew up together. I've known him since I was a teen, and even though I was closer to Mario, I know I can trust Thiago.

"Perhaps," I admit. "I think she needs to see the place where I lost my parents, just for her to understand how difficult it's been. Her father wasn't killed in her childhood home, so it's slightly different."

"I think this girl is getting to you, Boss," Mario says, and I can tell he's happy about it because his grin says everything. As we got older and reached a certain age, girls had become a focus for us, but I never once had a relationship. Nothing ever lasted longer than a few weeks at best.

"My father wanted this for me," I tell them both. "Instead of fighting it, I may as well embrace it. He chose this girl, and I need to know why."

"Maybe the answer lies in the office," Mario suggests gently. The sore spot for me is that room which I'm certain will always smell like death. Perhaps the blood that had stained the carpet will always be there. Maybe it's seeped into the floorboards.

"Once the party is over, I want a decorator to come in and completely redo the office," I tell Mario. "I want everything ripped out, right down to the shell, but not before I bring each man in there. I want them to sit in the space and absorb just what happened to Salvatore." My father's name on my lips tastes bitter, my chest tightening when I think about him. The ache will never go away, and I realize now, that's exactly what Luna is going through.

"Yes, Boss," Mario says, already on his feet with Thiago following behind. "I'll be in touch. Saturday?"

"Yes, we'll have the party on Saturday. Let's call it an engagement party for my new bride and me." They both nod, knowing smiles on their faces as they leave me to ponder which man could possibly be the one working for Tommaso. Perhaps our ghost will pay us a visit.

I pick up my phone and call the boutique which my mother owned. Two rings and the manager answers in her thick Italian accent. *"Buon giorno."*

"Silvia," I greet the older woman. "I need a dress for my fiancée, something..."

"Elegante?" she suggests.

"Si, and sexy," I inform her.

"Si, I can do this for you, send me the size and color. Delivery to your home, *signore."*

*"Per favo*r, Silvia, *grazie,"* I tell her before hanging up. I open an email and send her the photos of Luna, including her dress size, as well as underwear sizes. Everything will be in a royal blue, rich, elegant, and she will take the men's attention away from what they're there for.

Once I hit send on the email, I push to my feet and decide it's time to go home. I can work from there, but more importantly, I need to talk to Luna. She must be on her best behavior because the moment those men walk into that house, I want her to charm them. I know she can, she's done it with me, unknowingly.

Last night, being with her, inside her, taking her purity seems to have woken me up somehow. I can't explain it, but I feel alive for the first time in a long while.

When I walk into the apartment, the scent of baking hits me and I make my way to the kitchen to find Luna at the oven. "What are you doing?" I ask, confused at why she's staring through the dark window, which doesn't offer insight as to what is inside the oven.

Luna's gaze snaps to mine, her cheeks darken with a deep red and she smiles. "I was just making something for dessert," she tells me. "I wasn't sure if you we were going to have dinner?" The hope in her eyes makes my chest tighten.

"Why?" I don't know why I ask it, why I say it, but the moment the word falls from my lips, I want to pull it back. Not because I regret saying it, but because of the look on her face.

"I-I was just wondering," Luna whispers. "I'll be done here in a little while and be out of your way."

"You don't need to rush," I tell her, finding myself needing to be close to her. The scent of candied apples emanates from her as if she were the sweet treat. I make my way into the space, crowding her. "It's nice to see you in the kitchen," I taunt, knowing I'll get a rise out of the minx.

"Of course," she murmurs. "It's about the only thing I'm good for." Her words are pained. And before I can think about it, I grip her shoulders and spin her around.

"What do you mean?" I bite out, unsure of where the frustration is coming from.

Luna lowers her gaze to her entwined hands. When she lifts those glimmering orbs to mine, I find tears on her lashes. "The wife of a Boss is seen as the housemaid, the mother, the woman in the house. Not the person who stands beside her husband."

The pain in her tone squeezes at my chest. The feeling has been foreign to me. But since Luna's been in my life, I've come to realize it's affection. "That's not what I meant."

"Isn't it?" Her question is filled with hope, as if I could change her life, as if I could make her world brighter. That's what it's like when Luna looks at me, as if I were the hero in her story. But I'm not. And I cannot be both—hero and villain.

"Luna," I coo her name, cupping her cheek with my hand, reveling in her sweet, soft skin. "You're so much more than just a housemaid, you're more than anything you perceive yourself to be," I tell her earnestly, because fuck, she is a siren. And each time her voice invades my mind, I realize I'm falling deeper into her spell.

"Is that what you really think?" she asks in a tone that belies the anger that usually simmers between us. It's like she *wants* me. *Could she love a monster?*

"Yes, Luna." My admission says more than I want to admit, but I voice it anyway. She's drawn me in. Pulled me into the depths of her sweetness, and I have a feeling, I'm never going to get free.

"Thank you," she says, a small, innocent smile playing on her lips. For a lingering moment, I lean in and press my lips to hers. It's a strange feeling when you fall, when you leap off an edge you've been teetering on for so long.

I break the kiss and step away. "I'll be in my office." I leave her staring at my back because I can feel the heat of her focus, and I smile because for a short moment, I feel like a hero.

Each time we talk, I still find myself thinking back to what happened between our parents. I fight it. But between my growing affection for her, and my slowly diminishing hatred, it's as if I'm being tugged in two different fucking directions.

On one hand, I ache for a connection because

Luna is the only woman that I've been with who didn't shy away from my needs. But on the other, she's still the enemy's daughter.

However, I'm not sure if that matters anymore.

LUNA

HE WALKS OFF WITH A TORTURED EXPRESSION, AND I want nothing more than to talk about what happened between us, but I don't follow. Instead, I focus on the cookies I'd been baking. I needed to distract myself from last night, from the fact that Enzo owns me mind, body, and soul.

Denying it is no longer an option. I'm his. Even though we were to be married, I didn't expect to feel this connection to him. Last night should have scared me. Many times, since I first walked into his apartment should have scared me, but deep down, I crave his darkness like it's my own.

When his control slips, I want it. I ache for it. Perhaps my mind has been broken growing up in a mafia family. I flick off the oven and pull out the tray, setting it to cool before I head back into the studio to forget his frustration from earlier.

I pull off the jumper I'd been wearing, and shrug off my sweats. I always have a pair of tights and my leotard on just in case the opportunity to dance comes up. I kick off my sneakers and head for the stereo. I'm not sure what I want to do, but I know I need to clear my mind of Enzo and his whiplash emotions.

He's a storm, raging war on my mind and body, and it feels as if I'm caught right in the eye. A place that could be a safe place, but it could also be fatal.

The song that escapes the speakers has a deep bass, the thump vibrating through me as I move. My eyes close of their own accord, and I allow the rhythm to overtake me and lead me around the room. Deep down, I wish he was watching me right now.

I want him to see me. I want him to take me, slam me against the wall, and make me come. With every twirl, I breathe deeply, my core aching for what he delivered last night.

The thickness of him, spreading me, stretching me. How he toyed with me, lapping at my blood, tasting my very essence. As I move around the studio, my feet gliding as if I'm not even touching the ground, the images in my head play on.

My own dirty memories take hold and I realize

just how turned on I am. I spin around, my lungs work overtime as the crescendo hits me and I'm forced to come to a stop and my eyes snap open.

I thought Enzo was in the room. It feels as if his eyes are on me, but I'm alone. Staring at my flushed face in the mirror, I wonder what he thought of me last night. *Did I look beautiful?* I must have if he fucked me.

And as my chest heaves with deep breaths, I wish he would do it again. Make me feel pained pleasure as it courses through my veins. I ache for it. I squeeze my thighs together, the wetness obvious in my panties and I blush at myself.

The song comes to an end, and silence hangs in the air. Without thinking about it too much, I allow my feet to carry me down the hallway to his bedroom. Even though the door is closed, I ignore the fact that he may not want me in his space and push it open.

When I find the room empty, my brows furrow. But then I remember the office I spied a few days ago and head in that direction. The moment my steps hit the threshold, I'm shocked to find Enzo behind his desk, his hand on his thick cock, and his eyes on the door where I'm now standing.

He's not jerking off, just gripping himself as if he knew I was on my way. As if he were watching me all this time. He doesn't say anything, those dark eyes holding me hostage, reeling me deeper into the space.

"What are you doing?" The moment I ask it, I want the ground to swallow me. It's a stupid question because it's clear what he's doing.

"Were you looking for me?" His dark brow arches as he narrows his gaze. The man behind the desk isn't the same one who walked into the apartment earlier. I've not found Enzo my fiancé, I've found the monster who fucked me last night.

Squaring my shoulders for war, I nod. "I was."

"And what would my little dancer like?" The tone of his voice is husky, drenched with desire and lust. The need flickering in his stare has my blood heating and I take a few steps toward the desk.

"Why... Why are you...?" I wave my hand toward him, where he slowly releases his cock. "Were you doing that just to embarrass me?"

"Why would it embarrass you if I were jerking off?" he questions as if he's talking about the weather. "Did you want to do it for me?"

For a moment, I can only stare. There's something devilish in the grin Enzo offers me as he slowly unbuttons his shirt. Once the material flutters over his shoulders, I'm taunted by the smooth, tanned skin. His shoulders are muscular, wide, and his arms are tense when he moves and his belt clinks in the heavy silence of the room. He pushes to his feet and shoves his slacks down his legs.

"Would you be a good girl and kneel for me?" he asks, but it's tinged with danger. I watch as he steps out of his pants, and soon, all I'm looking at is the naked, Greek god of a man that will soon be my husband.

Without a word, I lower to my knees, but I tip my chin up with my shoulders squared as I look up at him from my vantage point. And I must be honest with myself, I've never seen a more beautiful man than Enzo de Rossi.

He moves toward me silently. When he stops inches from me, the hardness that juts from his hips is a hairsbreadth from my lips. I know what he wants. But he doesn't say a word, and he doesn't touch me. So, instead of waiting, I reach for his cock and wrap my hand around the shaft.

A hiss of pleasure escapes his lips when I stroke him. And when my lips wrap around the smooth, velvety head, my tongue laps at the arousal already on his cock. I keep my eyes on him, the power that burns through me at bringing a man like him pleasure makes my body turn hot.

I take him deep. The moment he hits the back of my throat, I choke, the saliva dripping down my chin, and that's when the monster loses control. His hands fist in my hair, his fingers gripping the strands, tugging until tears fill my eyes.

His dark stare locks on me. His focus is on his pleasure, and I'm merely the receptacle. He uses my mouth, pulling his cock free before thrusting along my tongue until he hears the soft gagging sounds which makes him smile.

"Such a good fucking girl," he hisses through clenched teeth. His hold on me is harsh, but I welcome the bite of pain. My leotard is soaked with spit, my nipples are hard against the material, and my panties are now drenched with my own arousal. When Enzo pulls free from my lips with a loud pop, the strings of saliva that connect us are what makes him chuckle. "My messy girl."

He tugs me to my feet, before spinning me around to face his desk. Behind me, his hand pushes down on my back lowering me front first, over the smooth mahogany veneer. The coolness of the wood causing goose bumps to rise on my skin.

"I hope you don't like this outfit," Enzo says in a low, feral grunt before ripping the pink material from my body. And then his fingers are inside me. Two digits dip into my core, deep, squelching causing my cheeks to burn. "So fucking wet for me already."

"Enzo, please fuck me," I plead, even though I know it's no use. If he's not ready, I'll have to wait. He doesn't respond, he only taunts me as he finger fucks me while his other hand reaches around my front to circle my clit.

Stars burst behind my lids as pleasure zips through every nerve-ending in my body. I claw at the desk, but there's nothing to hold onto. My thighs shake, my core tenses, and I'm about to leap over the edge when suddenly, a feeling of emptiness slams into me like a freight train.

"What the fuck?" I attempting to turn, to look at Enzo, but he holds me down against the desk and that's when I feel the cool metal as it slices the rest of my leotard until I'm naked before him.

"If you move, you'll get hurt," Enzo informs me, "Stay still, little dancer," he continues, and then it's when my skin tingles with the gentle touch of the tip of his knife. It trails down my spine, as if he's memorizing my body with the weapon that he uses to kill people with.

I should be scared.

I'm not.

He kicks my feet apart, and I lie forward, not moving, not breathing, because I am so focused on how it feels as it moves over me, I can't think about anything else. He toys with me as if I'm a puppet on a string as he trails the blade over the curve of my ass, before dipping between my thighs. The cold steel sending a shiver through me, and when Enzo pulls the blade away, he chuckles.

"Fucking delicious, all those juices dripping

over the knife I use to kill with." His voice is barely audible, a whisper filled with animalistic craving. Enzo's free hand tangles in my hair and he brings me to stand, before stepping back and spinning me to face him. "Tongue out." The two words are feral, and I obey instantly.

Gently, he places the wet metal over my tongue, and my flavor bursts on my tongue. The knife drops to the ground with a loud thud, and then Enzo crashes his mouth to mine. His tongue tangling alongside mine as we devour my arousal. His hands make their way to my hips before he grips my ass in a harsh hold before lifting me and placing me on the smooth desktop.

"Spread those pretty legs for me," he coos, his darkened tone causing a shiver of excitement to skitter down my spine.

I look up at him, locking my stare on his before I finally find my voice again. "Fuck me, please, Enzo." I'm a wanton slut for him right now, and I don't care. I'll own it. I'll admit it. And once we're done, I'll bask in it.

Seconds pass before he steps closer and nudges my entrance. The heat of him, the slickness of me, and then he's inside. Deep. Fully seated in my body, and the tension I'd been feeling earlier dissipates when he grips my hips and pulls back, before slamming into me.

It's not gentle.

It's not loving.

But it makes me see stars.

My toes curl with every thrust of his hips. His fingers dig into my flesh, and I know I'll be bruised. My hands tangle around his neck, and I pull him closer. My nails digging into his shoulders as I hold onto him.

Our bodies move effortlessly. As if we were made to fit together. His thick cock stretches me to my limit, but the agonizing pained pleasure is everything I crave. Those dark eyes pierce me, they hold me hostage. A connection I don't want to break.

Enzo releases one side of my hip and brings his hand to my throat. His thumb gently rubbing against my rioting pulse point. And then he squeezes. The tightness of his hold causes my body to pulse and his cock to throb. Everything becomes too much as my lungs struggle to pull in air.

I rake my nails down his back, and he only chuckles when I choke out a plea. His hips piston into me, fucking me, stealing every breath I cannot take, and seconds later, his other hand slides to my clit, and he pinches the hardened nub sending me into orbit.

ENZO

Stalking through the apartment, I push open Luna's bedroom door and find her still lounging in bed. Last night, I fucked her in my office, then once more in this bed, where she's now lying, holding up her Kindle as she reads.

The moment I step inside, she glances at me and smiles. "Good morning."

"I need you to be on your best behavior this weekend. On Saturday, I'm having a party and you need to be the entertainment." I stop inches from her bed and pluck the Kindle from her fingers before I tug at the blankets that cover her, but she grips them before I can expose her porcelain flesh. "We're going shopping for a dress."

Luna's eyes burn with fire before she scoots

up in bed and glares at me. "You know, I get that you hate me. And I totally get that my family are your mortal enemies, but after the things we did last night, I expect at least a fucking good morning before you order me around as if I'm one of your soldiers or capos." She drops her hands to her sides and the blanket she had been holding onto and I'm met with the sight of her tits. Delicious. Tantalizing. And utterly fucking mine. "Asshole," she bites out as she sways her hips while making her way to the closet.

The venom in her tone is warranted, so I don't punish her, but I do laugh out loud. "If I didn't like seeing my mark on you, I'd spank your ass for that outburst, little dancer." My warning doesn't go unnoticed when she peeks her head out from the walk-in closet.

"If you treated me like a human being, I wouldn't have to tell you that you're an asshole, and it wouldn't be true." Her sass makes my palm tingle, and I vow that the next time I get her naked, she'll get those pert cheeks brightened to a deep shade of red.

"We're leaving in ten minutes," I inform her, reminding myself of the task at hand.

When she appears once more, she's dressed in a pair of jeans and a flowing blouse that hides her bare tits. "Tell me something, Enzo," she says. "When did

I suddenly become someone you needed?"

I ponder her question, unsure of how to answer it because, I don't know if I need her. I could do this on my own. I could hire trusted women to walk in and do their job and leave at the end of the night. They would possibly offer me more than just the appearance at a party, but when I look at Luna, realization hits me that I prefer her.

Fuck Mario and him always being right.

"I don't need you, little dancer, but I do want you around."

Her mouth pops open in shock. "Why?"

I stalk toward her, needing to close the distance and inhale that candy apple scent that makes the inner monster rear its head and stake his claim. I grip her chin between my thumb and forefinger and tip her head so she's looking at me. "Because I love your tight little cunt around my cock, squeezing, milking, and pulsing for me to fill you up. I hunger to see your skin bruise with my mark. And I want to hear you scream my name every fucking day when I take all your holes and use them for my pleasure. I'm not the knight in shining armor in your romance, my little dancer."

I lean even closer, our lips so close, I could kiss her, and I know she wouldn't fight me off if I did. Even if she did, I would still steal her lips because they belong to me. I have fought this for so long, angry at my father for choosing her, but now I'm giving in. I've never done so before, and I won't ever do it again.

She's special.

She's unique.

And she's fucking mine.

"I'm the villain, and I'm proud to be. I want to be the monster you're afraid of, but I also want to be the monster that makes your body ache, tremble, and shake with profound pleasure. I'm the only person you will ever want or need."

"Enzo—"

"So, if you're looking for a hero, I'm not him. Instead, you found yourself someone who will fight to keep you safe. I'm not those fucking heroes in your books, I'm the one who will drench himself in blood for his queen. And I'll do it happily." I don't know why I'm telling her this. The admission has rendered me vulnerable, and it's not something I've ever done before.

Fear grips me, but I trust in my father. He chose this for me, and he must have known there was a reason for it. So, instead of hiding, instead of pushing her away, I allow her in, just for now. I need her to see the humanity. Just this one fucking second, I need her to believe me.

Slowly, those pretty, green eyes shimmer with tears before Luna blinks and the emotion trickles from her eyes. "I don't know what to say."

"Tell me you trust me," I throw back easily. For this plan to work, for me to be able to run the Familia the way my father would have wanted, I can't have a queen by my side, but also straddling the line between her past and present.

My family are everything to me, and in a few weeks, Luna will be a part of that life. She'll be the woman who will have to see me at my worst. There is no running away from this.

The corner of her mouth tilts. "I'm trying to." Her words are like a salve. It's not a yes, but she is trying, that's all I can ask for, at least for now.

"We'll work on it," I inform her. "Let's go." I step back, releasing her from my hold, before making my way to the door and into the living room. The dress I had delivered is in my bedroom, but I want to take her out of the apartment to test her loyalty. Maybe I shouldn't do it this way, but it's the only way I can be confident enough to trust her.

It's a gamble.

When you've lived this life for as long as I have, trust is not something to give out easily. Luna joins me in the foyer, and we make our way out to the elevator. The ride down is silent, and when we reach the car, I find Thiago waiting for me. His gaze lands on Luna for a split second before he offers me a nod, and we set off to the boutique.

At the sight of me, Silvia's face is etched in confusion. "Was it not—"

"Silvia," I interrupt her. "This is Luna Cavallone," I introduce my fiancée. "Nothing to worry about, she wanted to see the store," I tell Silvia, before dragging Luna off to the side and leaving Thiago to explain. I need my little dancer to feel at ease, and if I were to say anything more to Silvia, I have a feeling there would've been questions.

"These are incredible," Luna remarks as she heads straight for the evening dresses that shimmer on their hangers. I watch in wonder as her fingertips run along the soft fabrics. My body heating at the thought of her doing that to me.

For the first time, I want to take her into my bedroom, show her more pleasure than her body can take, and make her deliriously happy. But I shake it off, my focus needs to be on the interrogation on Saturday.

"You can choose any dress you'd like," I tell her, settling into one of the armchairs that overlook the dressing rooms. Luna glances at me from over her shoulder, a smile gracing her full, glossy lips.

"Any dress?" Her hand stops as she grips a hanger and pulls it from the rack. She disappears into one of the cubicles as Thiago joins me.

"Mario has it all set up. Each Capo will arrive within an hour of each other. They'll then join the

221

party in the living room. As they exit their vehicles, they'll each be led to the office, before joining the rest."

Nodding, I don't look over at Thiago, instead my focus is on the door that's slowly inching open. "Good. Now all we need is our entertainment." When Luna steps out of the change room, my breath is stolen.

She twirls in front of the full-length mirror before looking at me. "Does this please you, Mr. De Rossi?" Her taunting tone makes my dick throb against my zipper. Thiago's whoosh of breath beside me tells me this dress is the one. Even though I've already bought a dress for her, I know she's chosen the perfect one to lure every fucking soldier and Capo right into her net.

A siren.

Mine.

My fucking twisted obsession.

LUNA

I turn around in the mirror and take in my appearance.

The dress is beautiful, and I wonder if choosing it was the right decision. I'm still standing and staring at my reflection when Enzo walks into my bedroom. He doesn't speak, as he moves silently toward me, stalking me like a hunter does his prey.

When he's inches from me, his warmth at my back, he smiles. The sight of a man like him grinning is breathtaking. Handsome. Commanding. And utterly thigh-clenching.

"You look perfect tonight," he says, holding my shoulders and pulling me against his taut frame. " I never thought I would be so proud to walk into a room of my men with you beside me." There is an undertone of admission in his words.

"I thought you didn't do emotions," I utter, my voice scratching against my throat with every word.

For a short moment, he is silent, but then he leans in, sweeping my hair to the side. The motion sends goosebumps skittering across my skin. Enzo presses his lips to the nape of my neck, in a kiss so affectionate, so filled with emotion, my heart stutters.

"I don't," he tells me, whispering along my flesh. "But for tonight, I'll allow you to see me." When his eyes land on mine in the mirror, a lump slowly forms in my throat. Tears burn my eyelids, but I fight them off. I cannot cry, not because I'm with him, but because if I do, it may break the spell.

He is no longer a Boss seeking revenge looking at me.

He is not a man hellbent on making my life hell in the reflection.

Instead, I see him.

Enzo de Rossi.

A broken-hearted son.

The man I'm falling for.

And deep down, I wish, I pray, and I bargain with God, for him to love me back.

I'm nervous.

I haven't been in a gathering like this since I was a child, and even then, I had my father to protect me. Even though Enzo has claimed me, I don't know how he'd react if they were to taunt me with their jeers.

I'm still in enemy territory, and the man in charge hates my family to the point of obsession. A twisted obsession that's grown over the years. As the car moves up the drive, I'm speechless at the beautiful estate that we're on. I take in every glimpse I can get, until we stop outside a three-story home that is lit up in soft yellow light.

The black, wrought-iron balconies on the first and second floors are sculpted in the shape of vines, while the doors that lead out offer up a welcoming shimmer of gold. Enzo opens my door and offers me his hand which I gratefully accept.

"Thank you." Every time he touches me my skin warms, and my blood heats in my veins. My heart pitter patters, reminding me of just what kind of effect he has on me. Even though I try to tamp it down, I can't. It's a losing battle. And that scares me.

"Tonight, you're mine. Any time someone speaks to you, you reply with grace and elegance, but if any of these men touch you, come to me. I will make sure they understand the error of their ways."

"You mean kill them?" I challenge easily. With

every comment I throw at him, I notice how Enzo's stare darkens and how his mouth tilts into a wolfish grin. It's as if he's counting each of my missteps and logging them for use later on. If I'm right, I'm in for the punishment of a lifetime.

"That's for me to know," he informs me before we step into the house. Mario is behind us, along with the other guy, Thiago, who had accompanied us to the store when I got this dress. The sleek, floor-length black material hugs my curves. A slit runs from my ankle to my upper thigh. In front, the dip between my small breasts opens all the way down to my belly button. With long-sleeves, I'm warm, but still shiver when a few of Enzo's soldiers take me in with hungry gazes.

Enzo told me this was meant to be an engagement party, but I'm not stupid. I have a feeling this has a lot more to do with Valentino and the death of his father's lawyer than our upcoming nuptials.

He leads me through the house which I take in silently. When he leans in, he whispers, "I haven't been back here since I found my parents killed in my father's office." I don't look at him, but the pain in his words lances my chest. "It's easier that I'm not alone."

His admission has me snapping my attention to him. He's looking straight ahead, but I've stopped, causing him to turn toward me. The way his dark eyes flicker, hurts my heart. I don't know when I became so in tune with him, but it's as if his pain is mine.

"Why did you want to have this party here?" I whisper, but I know the two men behind us can hear every word. Mario's stare burns through me, and the reminder of what he said to me when I first arrived at the penthouse rings in my mind *perhaps you can change the man he is.*

"We all have to move on from our past," Enzo admits. "It's not easy, not by any means," he says before cupping my cheek. "But if we're brave enough, there might be more to this life."

"You can't go from hating me one day to feeling something the next," I inform him, still unable to believe that a man like him *can* change. Maybe I'm not giving him the benefit of the doubt, perhaps it's fear, me holding onto those first few days I spent around him. Whatever it is, I need him to know that the whiplash is exhausting.

Enzo nods slowly. "I know. I didn't say I love you, little dancer, but my anger is slowly dissipating." He smiles. "Tonight, I will introduce you as my fiancée. The woman who will become queen in my family, so I expect you to act like it." *And the asshole is back.*

"Understood," I sass, with a coy smile. We make our way into the living room which leads out onto a patio. The furnishings are antique, with

227

dark wood and brown fabrics. Everything about the space screams money, with gilded chandeliers dripping with diamonds and paintings that I'm sure cost more than an average person earns in one year.

There are already a few men with tumblers of whisky when we reach the outdoor patio, and when they turn to Enzo, I can tell they're happy to see the man beside me. The way their eyes flicker between me and Enzo, their expressions changing from smiling to serious sets me on edge.

"Cristiano, Franco, this is my fiancée, Luna," Enzo says.

The moment he tells them this, they offer a smile. "I'm Franco Moretti," the older man says. He must be in his late thirties, possibly early forties from the smattering of silver in his black hair. "It's lovely to finally meet the woman who's tamed Enzo."

"I'd hardly say I've tamed him," I inform the gentlemen who takes my hand and places a kiss on my knuckles. "Perhaps the better word is distracted."

Both men laugh. Cristiano steps forward to take my hand. "I'm Cristiano Russo, Franco's cousin." His introduction is slightly more seductive than Franco's because his lips linger just a moment longer than necessary on my knuckles, and he holds onto my hand, just a second more than he should.

"Stop with the antics, Russo," Enzo's voice is amused, but I can read the threat behind it.

Thankfully, he releases me at Enzo's words, and I'm tugged into the crook of my fiancé's arm. "I have a few of the men coming in this evening, an hour apart. I know it's a long time, but I needed it."

"Understood," Franco says. "I have spoken with the men at the dock. Shipment is arriving just after midnight, there's been a delay, so we don't need to rush."

"What shipment?" I ask, and all five men pierce me with a stare. Turning my attention to Enzo, I notice he's not happy that I voiced my question, but I want to know what's happening if I'm meant to stand beside him.

"It's nothing you need to worry about," Enzo informs me. "By the time I have to go to the docks, you'll be home safe." His hand trails down my back before he grips my ass in a harsh hold that causes me to gasp. I know Mario and Thiago can see what he's doing, but neither of them reacts. Not that I expected them to.

"Enzo," Mario's voice cuts through the tension. "They're here."

Dark eyes glance at me. "Have a drink, spend some time with Franco and Cristiano, and remember what I said." He presses his lips to my forehead before disappearing with both Mario and Thiago, and I'm left with the two new men I've just met.

"It's interesting to see Enzo so possessive over

his enemy's daughter," Franco remarks with a smile. "I honestly didn't think he'd ever come to terms with what his father did."

I turn to the older man after watching Enzo walk toward the entrance again. "Neither did I," I tell him honestly. "Have you known him for a long time?"

"All his life," he says, a smile on his handsome face as he lifts the tumbler to his lips and takes a long sip. But his eyes never leave mine. "My Familia and his have worked together for as long as I can remember, and even before that."

"Loyalty is everything," Cristiano chips in, his gaze drinking me in, just the way he slowly swallows his whiskey. "I'm sure you know all about that." He tips the glass toward me, before walking off, leaving the fragrance of his cinnamon and woodsy scented cologne behind.

"Ignore him," Franco tells me. "He doesn't take well to new people."

"Or to those who are enemies with his friend?" I ask, my brow arching in question, which earns me a rumbling chuckle from Franco. I've heard of the Moretti family. Three brothers lost their father when they were much younger. The eldest, Franco, took over, and runs the clan, and his two brothers are Capos in different cities, running the operations from afar.

"You're an intelligent girl," Franco remarks.

"Perhaps I should take you with me to LA, teach my ladies a thing or two."

"Your ladies?" Shock must be painted on my face because he laughs out loud.

Nodding, he closes the distance between us. "Yes, I like to have something beautiful to look at while I work. I have two assistants. Purely platonic." Even though I would usually doubt when a man tells me that, with Franco, I believe it's true.

"Then perhaps one day I'll visit," I tell him, and he offers me his arm which I accept. At least, there's one man here who kind of likes me. Now all I have to do is play along as Enzo asked.

ENZO

Leaving Luna with Franco and Cristiano calms me somewhat. They're connections I've known all my life, and I know Franco will look after her. Pushing open the door to my father's office has my lungs struggling to pull in air. The stench of death hangs heavily in the space as I step into it.

Nothing has changed, bar for the shampooed carpet and a new chair. Mario is behind me, his presences a force to be reckoned with.

"It's all still the same," I say, my voice lower than usual, but I know he hears me. I move deeper into the room and allow my fingertips to trail along the furniture as I step closer to the desk. I stop in front of it. The large wooden piece of furniture sits unchanged as if it's never seen the devastation that

232

I have.

"Are you sure you're okay to do this?" Mario asks as he stops beside me. His worried gaze rests on me, calming. "We can choose another venue."

"No." I shake my head. I'm adamant it has to be here. "I'm fine." I settle in the chair that's been perched behind my father's desk, and I wait. It doesn't take long for the door to open and the first of the Capos, Flavio, walks in.

His eyes flick around the room, taking in the space and I can tell he's scared. His hands fist and release at his sides as he notices small nuances about the office. I can't deny there is something about his reaction that has me on edge. I offer a nod to Mario, before I smile at the capo.

"Have a seat." I gesture to the chair in front of the desk, and he slowly drops into it. His dark eyes rest on me, watching, waiting, and I wonder if there's something more I'm supposed to do because, he seems out of sorts. "Do you know why you're here?" I ask as I take my seat.

He shakes his head, but his eyes never rest on one place. They dart around as if he's trying to see where the attack is coming from. Usually, I'd put that down to who we are and what we do, but he's one of ours and he's stressed. More so than he was in the board meeting.

"I am honestly unsure of what this is about."

His response is stifled, a whisper filled with fear.

"This was my father's office," I tell him, ensuring I leave enough silence for him to fill, but when he doesn't respond, I continue, "It was the room I found him, and my mother slain by the Cavallones."

"I'm so sorry for what happened," he finally finds his voice. "This wasn't the way I imagined our Boss would go," he tells me before shifting in his seat. He is uncomfortable, more than I imagined any of the men who work for me would be.

"Is there anything you'd like me to know?" I link my fingers, resting my hands on the desk as I lean forward, my focus on the man before me. "Because there are a few things that just don't add up."

When his gaze snaps to mine, the fear is palpable. I may be the boss, taken over from my father, but they have never seen me in action, not until Valentino, and I wonder if that instilled more fear than I imagined it would.

I've spent my life as the Familia's fixer, ensuring the people who needed to pay, did so in either cash or blood. But none of the men have ever witnessed me while I worked. Granted, I was harsh on Valentino, but then again, he deserved it. I don't dole out punishment unless it's earned.

Luna comes to mind for a split second before I shrug it off and focus on my new captive. He doesn't look like he's ready to party after this, but his reaction is a sign. One I've read all too well. I offer a small nod in Mario's direction, and he responds with his own signal. Flavio will be led down to the basement for more questioning.

For now, I'm done.

"I'll escort you out," Mario tells Flavio before he leads him to the hallway, and they disappear. Silence surrounds me, until I notice Cristiano at the doorway. I motion for him to enter.

"Your fiancée is rather fetching," he tells me as he settles in the chair opposite the desk. "I think there is something more going on with her though."

"Oh, and what makes you say that?" I challenge, my hackles rising as he questions Luna. If he came to me weeks ago, I would've considered it, but now, after what she and I have shared, I don't think of her as a threat any longer. She's more than that. She's mine.

"I think there is more to the girl than meets the eye," he informs me, but doesn't explain further. Frustration ebbs through me when the door opens. Mario gestures that the next man is here. "I'm around until you're done, come find me." Russo rises to his feet and makes his way out of the office, leaving me questioning everything I've come to believe.

She's not been perfect. Who truly is? Still, Cristiano has given me more to think about, more to consider about who she is, why my father chose her, and what she wants from our marriage.

When Marco walks in, I sit back and watch him saunter confidently to the chair opposite the desk. "Your father's sanctuary," he remarks as he settles in. He looks as comfortable as if he were in his own space. It doesn't at all look like the man is sitting in the same room his boss was murdered in. There's no regret, no guilt, and certainly no remorse in his eyes.

"And you're here to answer a few questions because I don't believe any of my Capos want me in this seat," I tell him without breaking my stare on the man before me. "I need to know who is loyal."

He snaps his gaze to mine. "You know I would lay down my life for you," Marco informs me easily, his face nothing but serene as he tells me this. Any tells of lying are out the window, because Marco is calm, and collected. But deep down, I wonder if that's something I need to be wary of and dig deeper into.

"My father needed that but didn't get it," I say, my voice calm, controlled, and deep down, just for a moment, I wish Luna was here. I'm not sure why she would aid me in my questioning, but I want her beside me.

"He was a man I spent my life looking up to," Marco tells me, causing me to look up into his earnest gaze. "I was a child when he stepped up to the leader role, to Boss." He leans forward, his elbows on his knees, and he matches my stare with one of his own.

"And you knew he was murdered, and yet, you had not reached out to me. You never once acknowledged that you were still behind us," I throw out, still unsure of what I'm dealing with. At first, I thought this would be easy, but the more I delve into the minds of these men, I realize there's so much more they're holding back.

"Your father was an icon. He was the Boss," Marco reminds me of something I don't need recapping. "And when someone of his caliber dies, we as Capos, we step aside to allow family to take over. We can't just walk in here, as if we own the place, because this is now your domain."

"And that's what you believe?" I challenge, needing more than just his words.

Marco nods, his expression filled with pain. His eyes lock on mine and I read the heartbreak in them. "Salvatore was everything, he was like a father, and mentor to me." His words hit me right in the chest, and I pray Mario is listening, because right now, fucking emotions have taken a hold of me, and I blame Luna. She's opened this box and left me vulnerable. "He was the man I looked up to since I was a kid. He was the reason I took the oath."

"I understand," is all I can muster. This is harder than I anticipated. I thought just questioning these men would lead me to the bastard who's feeding Tommaso the information, but now I've learned that's not true.

When he leaves, I'm met with another of our Capos who offers me the same speech. I only have one more man to see and ask Mario for a moment to get my bearings. There has been too much said in the past few hours.

"Luna is here," Mario says before stepping aside. I glance up to find my fiancée at the threshold of the office. I didn't want to bring her in here because it was a sacred space. One her family tainted, but the moment she steps inside, it feels as if I can breathe again.

"My father taught me something when I was growing up," she informs as she strides up to the desk. For a split second, I want to hurt her, to make her cry as she learns about the room that she's in. I want to make her bleed. To see that pretty crimson on her porcelain thighs as I fuck her mercilessly.

But I don't.

I tip my head to the side, regarding her with interest. "And what is that?"

"To read people when they're lying," she informs me, and I realize there were multiple times over the past few weeks I'd lied to her. "I can tell from the moment someone walks into a room, to the moment he or she walks out, that they're not telling the truth."

"And you're informing me of this when I'm bringing in the last man in my questioning?" I challenge her. My face must be a picture of disdain and frustration.

"Yes, because this is the only man who is new to your family," Luna informs me easily, as if she already knew that he would be the one working for her uncle. As if she is here because of him. My nerves are shot, and my rage intensifies when she stalks around the desk. "I'm not a spy. You stole me from my family, but this man..." she leans in, allowing her lips to trail over my ear. "He's the one that I don't feel comfortable around."

My eyes meet hers. "And you expect me to trust you?"

"If you don't, you may end up in that chair with blood drenching the carpet," she informs me of a moment I would rather forget. My hand grips her neck, holding her by the delicate column as I bring her closer. Before I can say anything more, Luna whispers, "Word gets around. Questioning them in the same room that they probably know like the back of their hand isn't going to help."

Her words sink in slowly, and that's the moment I realize my father didn't choose the woman only for her beauty, it was for her intellect.

"Then show me, little dancer, "I coo in her ear,

earning me a soft shiver from the woman who will soon wear my ring, bear my name, and give birth to my heirs. He didn't realize I would accept this; I know that. My father knew I would fight tooth and nail, but for me to finally come to terms with making Luna my wife, probably wasn't on his radar.

"I'd be happy to, she informs me before slipping around the desk and sliding onto my lap. I don't know how I'm meant to question the last of my Capos like this, but I'm going to leave it to my future wife.

LUNA

I can't believe he's allowing me to sit in on this meeting. Or better yet, interrogation. He's tense, I can feel it in his shoulders as he allows me to slip onto his lap. His hands grip me tightly, holding on as if he needs my presence to ground him.

"No talking," he whispers quietly. His hand squeezes my hip, and I know it's a warning for me to be silent. But I'm confused by his actions. Enzo is not a man to do something without a plan. There must be a reason he's keeping me here when he's going about his business.

I lean against him before asking, "Why allow me in here if I'm not meant to talk?"

Enzo glances at me, his lashes fluttering on his cheeks before he leans and murmurs in my ear,

"Perhaps having you here will jolt his memory. Nothing like a pretty girl to make a man talk more than he should." On one hand, I understand that, but I can't deny my annoyance is through the roof. But instead of responding, I sigh as the door opens and an older man walks in. He looks vaguely familiar. However, I know I haven't formally met him before.

When his gaze lands on me in Enzo's lap, his eyes widen, but the flicker of shock is quickly quelled. "Enzo," he says as he settles in the chair opposite the ornate desk. "You need your fiancée to do business?"

A chuckle reverberates through Enzo's chest. "Not at all, but she'll soon be my queen, and she needs to know what's going on within the Familia."

"What is going on?" the older man asks as he rests his ankle over the opposite knee. He doesn't seem at all perturbed at being in the office, but each time his eyes flicker to mine, it's with familiarity. As if he knows me. But I can't recall where I've seen him.

Perhaps he knew my father. Enzo responds, breaking my thought process, "There are a few things I need you to tell me, Giuseppe," he pauses for a moment before continuing, "You've been receiving payments in an offshore account for the past eight months. You've also been seen with Valentino when he was known to be working with Tommaso. The time frame makes me think you may have had something to do with my parent's murder."

"How dare you accuse me of such a blasphemous thing!" The older man's face turns dark with rage. His wrinkles creasing further as he scowls at us.

"Is that why you recognized my soon to be wife the moment you walked in?" Enzo challenges, keeping his cool. The man is like a robot when it comes to his business, no emotions tinge his voice. "Because I can read a liar from a mile away. And you, Giuseppe, smell like a rat."

"Whatever you think you know is purely coincidence. I've never—"

Enzo's grip on my hips tightens, his fingers holding me as if I were his life raft and he's about to sink into the depths of his anger. "Coincidence?" His voice only now taking on a violent grit that makes my spine tingle. "What we found doesn't add up to just some random mistake," he informs the older man who is glaring at me.

"I have nothing to do with that bastard," he spits, "Cavallone was nothing more than a means to an end."

"Oh?" Enzo says, his interest piqued. "I'd like to know what end you're talking about, because if it was the death of my mother and father, then you will pay the ultimate price for your disloyal actions."

"I-I had nothing to do with it." He pushes to

his feet, but Mario is already behind him, his hand on Giuseppe's shoulder, shoving him back into the chair. "It's all a lie. I had nothing to do with the deal."

It feels as if Enzo is trying to bruise me with the way his fingers flex into my hip. "Oh? And what deal was that?" His tone like steel, cold and hard, and I pity the man before us. I know he'll die. And it will be by Enzo's hand. I don't blame Enzo because this is what is expected. If you're not loyal to your Familia, then you deserve to be taken out. The vow uttered when a Made Man is brought into the fold, is sacred. It's like a wedding vow. Once you promise your life to the clan, there is no getting out. It's not only that, but you also pledge your loyalty, and your support, no matter what.

Those who break the vow die.

Death before dishonor.

Giuseppe's face creases, guilt shining in his eyes as he looks at his Boss. He may be older than Enzo, but that means nothing in this situation. And he knows it. There will be no mercy.

"Tommaso contacted Valentino," he admits, his gaze flickers to mine before returning to Enzo's. "At first, I didn't want to do it. The De Rossi Familia was mine, I belonged here. I've been a Capo for years, and it's been rewarding."

"So, you decided to join forces with our mortal enemy and help murder my parents? Your Boss?"

Enzo asks incredulously. "Is that how you *belonged*?"

"No. No. It wasn't like that. My payments were decreasing, I needed the money. You don't understand, Enzo. I was struggling." The plea in the older man's voice makes my chest ache, but what I don't understand is why he didn't go to Salvatore, surely Enzo's dad would have helped one of his own.

"Salvatore did everything for his Capos, I knew that because I watched him do it. He believed in family, in loyalty. My father was a man with integrity, even if he made deals which brought us some heat from the feds from time to time. We couldn't stop the fact that some things needed to be done under the table, but, he would never let his men fall for no reason."

My lungs hurt as I try to breathe. It seems Salvatore was just like my father. He loved his men, his family. He did bend over backwards for them, making sure they had everything they needed for the businesses to run smoothly.

The older man shakes his head profusely, but I know it will do nothing to afford him mercy. There is no way what he's done can be forgiven. "Enzo, you don't understand—"

I'm pushed to my feet gently, the movement causing Giuseppe to stop speaking. His eyes widen when he realizes what's about to happen. Enzo is at full height as his hand slowly releases me. He doesn't rush at Giuseppe. The slow, predatory way he takes his steps has ice racing through my veins. But I don't cower, I'm too enthralled by my fiancé to be scared. His hand reaches for the knife I know is hidden at his belt. He pulls it from the thick leather sheath.

"I wanted each of my Capos to know what happens to men who are untrustworthy, who double-cross me. I showed you that when I brought all of you to watch as I made a spectacle of Valentino. I don't feel an ounce of guilt for it." When Enzo speaks, his voice is devoid of emotion. Not even anger.

Mario's gaze flits to mine as he tips his head to the side. He regards me with interest, as if he's waiting for me to run. But I've watched Enzo do this before. I don't understand why he's so concerned for me.

"Tell me the truth," Enzo commands the man before him. "Tell me the real reason you went to Tommaso and not my father. Because there has to be more to the story."

When Giuseppe doesn't speak, the sleek, silver blade glints before it slices along his cheek, from his left eye down to the corner of his mouth. The older man does not dare move. A cry of pain bounces off the walls of the office as Enzo waits.

"I-I..." he shakes his head, blood dripping from his face as he looks up at Enzo. "Please, don't do this." I'm not sure why he even bothers asking because he knows there's no longer hope. "I-I can't."

"But you can, Giuseppe," Enzo taunts the man, slicing along the right side of his face. It's not overly deep, but it sure makes a mess on Giuseppe's crisp white shirt. "Tell my fiancée and I what you did."

My ears prick when I hear Enzo's words. "What?" I can't stop the shocked response from falling from my lips. "What do you mean?" I step forward, but Enzo holds up his hand, stopping me in my tracks.

"Look at her, and tell her the fucking truth," Enzo grits, his voice turning darker, more dangerous. When he gets like this, I know there's no going back. There will be a lot of blood spilled tonight. I glance at the older man who's now looking at me as if he's pleading for mercy.

"What is he talking about?" I ask Giuseppe, my hands fisting at my sides. I don't want to panic, but when his lip trembles, and Enzo presses the knife to his eye, I shiver.

"I gave you an order, Giuseppe. The last one you'll ever get because after this, you will meet your maker." The promise is there. He doesn't have long to live. I'm tempted to go to him and shake him. I want to force him to speak.

But when he does, I want him to take the words back. "I killed your father, and I killed. Salvatore because that is what Tommaso wanted." His admission has me dropping to my knees as realization hits. My uncle wanted my father dead. He wanted to lead. My father being older than Tommaso, meant that he would be Boss until his death. And my uncle couldn't deal with being an Underboss.

Enzo turns to me, as he spins the weapon in his hand and offers it to me. The handle pointed down at where I'm kneeling. My hand trembles as I reach for it, gripping it tightly as my future husband grins manically at me.

"Time for you to earn your stripes," he tells me. "You're part of my family now." This isn't just him accepting me. He's telling me that I can rule beside him. If I do this, I become part of the De Rossi Familia, as the queen.

Pushing to my feet, I take the two steps that bring me to the man who killed my father. Everything I ever believed was a lie. But Enzo gave me the truth. Silently, I nod at Mario who holds Giuseppe down, keeping him steady as I cut away each button of his now stained shirt.

Once it falls open, I use the blade to carve my father's name in his chest. The cries of his pain are a melody I'll never get out of my head. Once finished,

I lower my hand and add Salvatore's name in blood against the flesh of a murderer.

When I've completed my task, I tip my head to the side and smile. "Goodbye," I tell him before handing the knife to Enzo who slices his throat slowly. The gurgle of the dying man fills the room. He chokes, sputters, and it doesn't take long for the light in his eyes to dim.

"Leave us," Enzo says as he looks up at Mario. His best friend nods and takes his leave. And that's when my fiancé turns to me, and I know what's coming next.

ENZO

Watching her torture Giuseppe has done something to me. I can't describe it, but my mind is focused on claiming her. At first, I thought she'd shy away. I wanted her to tell me she couldn't hurt someone. But the moment he admitted to killing our parents, I saw her change and it made my dick hard.

"You realize you're a De Rossi now," I tell her when I turn to her. My gaze focused on her cheeks which darken with a shade of red. "You may not have taken the vow, but that was as good as it gets."

Luna tips her head up, her eyes locked on mine as she regards me with a small smile. "I was a De Rossi from the moment my uncle signed the contract." Her words make me grin, and I'm sure I look fucking scary as I stalk toward her. With every step I take, she takes one back and soon, her ass hits the edge of the desk. In the dim light of the room, even with the party in full swing just outside, there's electricity zipping between us.

"And you're okay with that?" I ask, it's a challenge for her to refuse me. To tell me she still hates me as much as I want to hate her. But the moment she took my knife, I realized I'm falling for her. But it's too soon to be admitting those words to her. It's not me. I'm not a man who ever wanted forever. Instead, I craved one-night stands where I didn't have to see them again.

Luna nods slowly. "I am." Her admission is a whisper of confidence which settles in my chest, warming me from the inside out.

"You'd love a killer?" I test the waters. *Tell me no. Tell me no.* She's too innocent for me, for this world. I still believe that even after what I witnessed tonight. She may have carved a man's flesh, but the girl before me is still just that—a girl.

Luna offers me an almost shy smile. I say almost because there is fire dancing in her pretty gemstone eyes. They look almost magical, as if drawing me into their depths, reminding me of the two sides of my personality—man and beast. I'm certainly no hero, not at all a knight in shining armor, but Luna doesn't want that, she's made it clear.

"Most girls want a pretty white dress, a castle

on a hill with perfectly manicured gardens. They want the perfect life filled with roses and rainbows. I've never been one of those girls," her words are confident. Her admission makes my cock throb against my zipper. "I've been that princess," she says then. "I grew up with people waiting on me hand and foot. I was told daily how perfect I am, how beautiful I am."

"And now?" I nudge, wondering where she's going with this. If she doesn't realize it yet, she better learn quickly. I'll most certainly make sure she never forgets just how exquisite she truly is.

"And now I'm ready to be a queen," she offers before taking a step toward me, but there's not very far to go. Our bodies are flush against each other. Her tits pressing against my chest, her curves fitting against the hardness of my torso.

I don't say a word. Instead, I grip her hips and lift her onto the desk. I don't ask, instead, I shove her legs wide. The slit in her dress allows me access to her panties which are soaked.

With two fingers, I tease her core against the material now slick with arousal. "I think you like being a bad girl," I murmur as I lower my mouth to hers. But I don't kiss her. I merely taunt her lips with mine. "Deep down, you've always known that. Even when you fought me when you arrived at my apartment, you knew there was no way out. But you didn't want one. Did you?"

Luna tips her head to the side, her long lashes fluttering against her cheeks as I tug her panties to the side and find her dripping cunt. Her smoothness is slick, slippery, and my two fingers easily slide inside her. A whimper of pleasure tumbles from her plump lips.

"I did want to escape." Her confession has me stilling my hand, but the naughty girl rolls her hips, her hands gripping the edge of the desk as she fucks herself on my fingers. "I wanted to make you realize that you're also prone to emotions. I wanted you to realize no matter how much blood is on your hands, you're still human."

Then, before I have time to respond, Luna grips my wrist in her delicate fingers, and moves my hand against her while undulating her hips. Her head drops back as her face contorts with pleasure. A cry of bliss escapes her mouth and I steal it with my own. Our tongues dance a duel and I know there's no way this woman is ever getting away from me.

Her arousal drenches my palm. My fingers are gripped by her slick walls, and my cock weeps at the sensation. I pull my hand from her, bringing both digits to her lips. I paint the sweet juices that glisten on my hand over her lips making them wet with her pleasure.

And then her hands are on my belt, my zipper,

and even though there's still a dead man inches from us, I thrust into Luna's waiting cunt. Balls deep. Fully fucking seated in my fiancée's pussy.

I steal her mouth once more, tasting her as I deepen our connection. Her hands twine around my neck, pulling me closer as her legs wrap around my waist. I've never done this before. I've never once fucked a woman beside a man who's bleeding out.

But my cock has never been harder.

"Open your eyes, little, dancer," I growl, my voice feral and animalistic and my girl snaps her gaze on mine. "I want you to look at me while I do this. While I make you come all over my cock, I want you to know exactly who is inside you."

Her body pulses, and she pulls her fat bottom lip between her perfectly straight teeth and bites down hard as I grip her neck. When I notice the trickle of blood forming between her pearly whites, I can't help but smile.

"Good girl," I coo before lapping at her, tasting the crimson fluid. My body burns hot, and I don't stop fucking her, harder, and harder, deeper, until her nails are digging into my shoulders.

"Please, please, I need to come," Luna pleads. Her words like an aphrodisiac to me because I throb inside her, and I'm sure I'm stretching her to her limits because she winces, but there's still a smile on her lips. I squeeze her neck tighter, stealing every breath she struggles to pull in. I dip my other hand between us, and circle her clit slowly, torturing her. With every movement, she tightens around my cock as if she's trying to milk every drop out of me.

"That's it, little dancer," I coo, brushing my lips against hers. "Come for me. Drench my cock with those sweet juices of yours." Her body convulses, her cunt pulsing, and I know she's close.

"Fuck, Enzo, please," her choked plea is music to my ears, and I realize this little dancer has fucked my life upside down, and I'm okay with it. I've hated her family for so long, but right now, all I want is to own her pleasure.

I pinch her clit hard, before dipping two fingers inside her feeling my cock sliding in and out, and I open her to the point of her crying out through her husky voice.

"Come for me." And she fucking does.

"Enzo!" My name is a scream as I release her neck and Luna soaks me right down to my boxer briefs. Her body pulsing around me is too much and I thrust once, twice, and a third time before I release my orgasm deep in her body.

I slowly pull out of her and help her fix her outfit before zipping my slacks. I step back and cup her face so she's looking at me. "Time for me to go do some bad things, little dancer," I tell her with a soft kiss to her lips. "I want you home, Thiago will drive you and make sure you're safe."

Luna shakes her head. "I want to be there."

"No." My voice is firm, a no-nonsense tone that I have a feeling my dear little dancer will not obey. But I will happily tie her up, put her in the car, and make sure Thiago takes her home.

"You said I was—"

"I said you were to go home. I don't like disobedience, Luna." My use of her name makes her eyes widen. "I cannot go to the pier knowing you'll be in danger."

"But you'll be in danger," she throws back easily, and I can't deny she's right. I'm not sure what is coming when we reach the harbor, but with the shipment on its way, I must finish off this bullshit Irish mob business that's so clearly taking over the Familia in New York. And with Moretti, and Russo here, I'll have the backup I need.

"I am in danger every day of my life, my sweet," I tell her. "It doesn't change just because I'm at the harbor, or in my car, or even in a fucking restaurant. And what happened to you hating me?" I challenge. I'm not sure why I do, perhaps it's because I want her to say the words—she doesn't hate me.

"Hate is a strong word," she admits. "Perhaps I'm just a little obsessed." Her taunting tone heats my blood once more, but I can't take her again. When her eyes land over my shoulder, I know Mario is here. I turn to find my right-hand man standing on the threshold of the office.

"We're ready."

I nod at his words. "Luna, please, just this one time, listen to me."

She tips her head to the side, arching a dark brow at me and her lips tilt into a playful grin. "Is that affection you have for me, Mr. De Rossi?"

A chuckle vibrates in my chest, and I shake my head. "I don't like killing innocent people." I tip my head to the dead man still in the chair. "And it seems you don't either."

"Perhaps," is her only response as I tangle my fingers with hers and lead her out of the office. I'm not nervous for tonight's festivities. Sadly, our engagement party turned into a bloody evening, but at least Luna now knows she's mine.

"Get the crew on that," I tell Mario as we pass him and he's already pulling out his phone before I have time to finish my sentence. By the time we reach the party, it's dwindled, thankfully, and I find Cristiano and Franco, along with the two younger Moretti brothers—Giovanni and Matteo.

"Time to go," Franco informs me before setting his glass down. Everyone is armed. Each man in this room is ready for a fight, and I turn to Luna, who's become mine in the time she's spent with me, and I know I want her safe.

"Go with Thiago," I tell her, and the man in question steps forward. He nudges his jacket out of the way and I see he's carrying as well. "Straight to the penthouse." My order is for him.

"Of course." He nods, and I let Luna go. I watch until they disappear, but I don't miss her casting a glance over her shoulder to look at me once more. The action has my chest tightening.

She's fucked with me.

She's made me feel.

And now, she can never walk away.

ENZO

T<small>HERE'S</small> <small>TENSION IN THE AIR AS WE MAKE OUR WAY</small> to the cars. Nobody speaks. We're an army going to war. I slip into the back of the SUV with Franco, while Mario takes the driver's seat. The convoy of cars that move out of the property would make any sane man crazy. Blacked out windows, sleek, shiny raven-hued metal, with men inside that could either make you cry or make you scream, most times, we do both.

"She's getting under your skin," Franco says, his voice stern, yet calm as if he's talking about the weather. I don't want to respond, so I leave his assessment to hang in the air for a while. "I can read you like a book, Enzo," he tells me.

"Perhaps," I answer, my gaze meets Mario's

in the rear-view mirror, and I can see the smile that creases the corners of his eyes. He's known me for so long, along with Franco, so they both probably think the same. "She's a good fuck," I tell Franco.

"You may say that now, but to send her home to safety means more in our world than just a good fuck," he says, before glancing at me. I can feel his stare piercing a hole right through me. When you've grown up in this life, you're taught to read people, to pick up on their tells, signs that they're nervous, uncomfortable, and uneasy. There is no doubt he can see past my façade of trying to play it cool.

"She is my fiancée. If I don't make sure she's safe, I'll mar my father's last wish for me to marry her," I say, but then smile. "Also, perhaps she's niggling at my defenses. There's something about the sweet, innocence that she exudes."

"I thought so." He nods slowly. "There's nothing wrong with wanting someone in your life, Enzo. A family."

"You can talk, you've been single for years. When are you going to take your own advice?" I ask, keeping my attention on him.

He shrugs. "At times, I think it's pointless." There's pain in his words, and I want to dig deeper, but I don't. Instead, I allow the silence between us. "Maybe one day I'll find someone who can put up with me." He chuckles while shaking his head.

"What about you Mario?" Franco asks my best friend. "Any pretty young things in your sights?"

"Not right now. My focus is the job." The conversation is light, carefree almost, considering we're about to stop a shipment of drugs from being brought into our city. It doesn't take us long to hit the pier, and once we're all parked and out of the cars, I'm tense once more. My shoulders tight with anxiety.

"This way," Franco leads, and we follow. Our steps echoing in the darkness. When we reach the warehouse, we're met by the rest of the Moretti clan, as well as more De Rossi men who are already armed with guns in hand.

The Irish have no idea we're here. And they're in for a surprise. I pull my knife from its sheath and grip it tightly. In my other hand is a Glock which I've only used a handful of times. The handle engraved with the De Rossi emblem.

"It's docking," a man tells Franco as we near the edge of the pier. The water below is tar black, licking against the wooden surface of the gangplank. We watch from the shadows as they lower the bridge of the ship, a handful of men making their way off the boat with heavy sacks of what I can only assume is the product.

"Wait until they've packed everything in the container," Franco orders. The men disperse quietly in the darkness, keeping to the shadows. It seems the Irish are clueless as they continue unpacking coke from the boat.

A man saunters down the gangplank and Franco stiffens. "Who is that?" I ask, but he only shakes his head. I don't continue my questioning because it's then we realize the ship is now empty of all the sacks. It's time we need to move. But the moment I push to full height, my gut clenches when I see Tommaso coming at us with a gun. The man who Franco recognized is also armed.

Bastard is working with the Irish.

And that's when all hell breaks loose.

My arm extends, my finger on the trigger. I keep my focus on one man and one man only. I leave the rest to our crew as I stop in front of Tommaso. It seems Valentino truly was a fucking bastard who turned on his family.

"Where is my niece?" Tommaso questions, his gun trained on me. I'm not afraid of dying, but the thought of leaving Luna utterly alone does something to my chest. I don't want to think about it any longer than I have to. I've fallen for the tiny dancer, and there is nothing I can do about it now.

All I need to do is survive this.

"She's at home, where she belongs," I tell him, a sly smile curling my lips. "And with any luck, she'll be having a baby in the next nine months." I know

I'm poking the bear, but I don't give a shit. This asshole will die today, and it will be by my hand.

"Like fuck she will," he spits angrily. "She is a Cavallone," he informs me while gunshots and shouting sound around us. It's like a war waging while we're having a fucking drink and chat. I don't know if Tommaso has told them not to come at me, but none of the Irish are even looking in our direction.

"Trust me when I tell you, she's never going to be a Cavallone again. She's accepted her fate, and so have I." If someone had told me I'd ever utter those words, I would have laughed in their face and told them they're lying, but as I say it, I know it's true.

"You think you can take what is mine?"

"I already have," I taunt, and that's when I pull the trigger, but I don't kill him. Not yet. I take a couple of shots at his torso, sending him to the ground with a loud grunt of pure agony. "I've never been one for flair, I like to end my enemies quickly, but you're special."

The bastard picks up his arm and takes a shot, hitting me in the shoulder. Pain causes me to groan, but I swallow back the words of revenge, and breathe through the agony. With a smile on my face, I walk closer, giving him a direct shot to my legs, but he can't take it because he's clawing at his knees which are bleeding out far too quickly.

"You fucking took my family!" Tommaso's voice is filled with venom, but I have a cure for his poison, it's my queen waiting for me back at the penthouse. "But I will take it all back from you."

I can't help but laugh out loud when he says this. "Can't take from the living when you're dead," I inform him before dropping to a crouch before him. I press the barrel of my gun against his forehead, right between his beady fucking eyes, and I say, "Time to meet your fucking maker."

"She will never be yours," are his final words before shots ring out and pain lances its way through me. Even though I have my bullet-proof vest on, the agony causes me to stagger back. I stumble as one of Tommaso's goons gets in my face while two others drag Tommaso away.

I look up at the bastard towering over me and I aim the weapon in my hand at his head and pull the trigger. Tommaso may have escaped me now, but I will find him. My confidence in what I have planned for him is brimming as I rise to full height.

My phone vibrates violently in my pocket, and when I pull it out, the words on the screen have my heart beating against my chest as if it were about to escape.

"Enzo! What the fuck?" Mario's voice catches my attention. His eyes are on my chest. A quick glance at my shoulder confirms I need a doctor, but that will have to wait because I need to help my men.

I've never feared death. I've danced with her night after night while working as Underboss for my father. And now that I'm in his seat, I still don't run from a fight, especially when it's my men that need me.

Familia forever.

Death before dishonor.

I race into the fray, my gun held high and pull the trigger as I run through the gunshots flying around me. I drop to my knees suddenly as pain skitters over me, and the warmth of metallic fluid spreads over my crisp white button up.

Weariness overtakes me and I can't fight it anymore.

My eyes flutter.

Screams and shouts echo around me.

And then darkness.

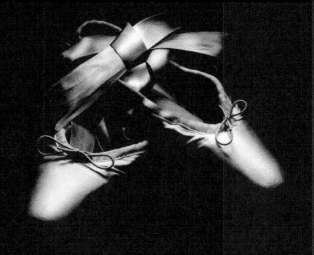

LUNA

My eyes snap open.

My lungs drag in air with difficulty as pain shoots through me like an electric current. I can't move my body. Turning my head forces an agonizing groan to tumble from my lips, and when I look around, I realize the soft yellow light isn't that of my bedroom at the penthouse, it's a hospital room.

Confusion settles in my mind which is clouded with memories that flit back and forth between past and present. The door swings open with a soft whoosh announcing the arrival of somebody.

"Jesus, Luna," the voice says. *His* voice says. I glance over, disappointment hits me right in the chest. It's not Enzo, instead I find Thiago hobbling over as he holds onto the crutches. "Are you okay?"

My brows furrow and it all comes crashing back with clarity that has my eyes watering. Tears threaten to spill, but I blink them back as I find myself wanting only to know where Enzo is.

I nod slowly.

I open my mouth to speak, but no words come out.

"He's on his way," Thiago assures me before I can get my question out. It's as if he's reading my mind. The machines that are plugged into the wall beep, a stark reminder of what happened.

"It hurts," I croak as more pain skitters over my body. My limbs are numb, as if they're no longer there. Fear grips my chest, squeezing painfully, but when I look down at the bed, I can see the shape of my legs, my feet, and relief washes over me.

"I'll get the nurse," Thiago informs me before leaving me on my own once more to ponder what the hell happened. We were in the car when I remember a bright light, two of them, blinding me. Thiago swerved out of the way, and if it weren't for him, I doubt I would be here now.

If I were sitting behind him in the car, I may also not be alive, but I'd chosen to sit on the other side so I could talk to him while leaning forward onto the passenger seat. It was his idea because he didn't want me up front. He told me I was important, and that meant I should feel as if I were being escorted home.

I recall laughing at that.

And then, the loud crash that hit the back of the car as if they expected me to be behind him. The aim was there. And then, crunching metal echoed around us, sirens, paramedics talking, and then I blacked out.

When the door opens again, it's with a loud crash making me wince at the sound. "Luna," my name is a shocked whisper, but this time it's not Thiago at the door, it's the man who has stolen my heart.

But when I look over at him as he makes his way toward me, my stomach drops to my feet. He's covered in blood. His shirt is stained, and he's bandaged around his middle.

"What happened?" My voice scratches against my throat, causing me to cough, choking on the dryness. Enzo is at my side, holding my hand, his fingers grip my trembling digits as he brings them to his lips. "What happened?" I ask again when he doesn't answer.

Those dark eyes that always capture my gaze, drop to the bed. He takes me in, from my feet up to my head, before landing on my stare. "Your uncle will soon be dead." His words are confident. There is no doubt in my mind Enzo will be the one to pull the trigger, and I nod in understanding.

I didn't expect him to live.

I don't think I wanted him to live while knowing what he did to my father, to Enzo's parents. He deserves what he gets. All I can hope is that it will be painful.

"There was an accident," I tell Enzo who's just staring at me as if I weren't real. The disbelief on his face slowly morphs as he glances over his shoulder to Thiago who's returning with a nurse.

The men don't speak as she works on my drip, then she injects something I'm guessing is pain killers into the tube attached to my arm. "This will make you feel better," she affirms, and I nod.

Once we're alone again, Enzo turns to Thiago. "What happened?" His voice is croaky. I'm almost certain he's about to pass out, but when he settles in the chair which overlooks my bed, I notice how he isn't moving his arm.

"A car came at us, fucking SUV, right out of nowhere." Thiago's tone is tinged with guilt, but it's not his fault. We both didn't see it coming. We were almost home.

"Enzo," I whisper, as Thiago helps me, holding the glass of water and the straw so I can take a long sip before I feel as if I can talk again. "What happened at the docks?"

"I'm more concerned at what happened to you," he throws back with a glare on the younger man.

269

"It's not his fault. Stop being an asshole," I choke out, once again, a bout of coughing making my chest hurt. Both men are at my side, a third joins them moments later. Mario is here, his hands on my feet, but for some reason, his touch is non-existent.

"How are you fee—?"

"Touch my leg," I whisper, fear turning my blood to ice.

"What?" All three men say at once.

Ignoring them, I look at Mario and say once more, "Touch my leg, my feet, something. Just touch me." My voice shrills as hysteria takes hold of me. "Do it! Do it! Touch my legs!"

The moment Mario obeys, and his hands land on my lower legs, panic sets in. I feel nothing.

"What's going on?" Enzo furrows his brows in confusion. "Little dancer, what's wrong?"

"I-I-I can't f-feel it." My voice sounds foreign to me. I don't recognize it, and I doubt the men do because the heartbreak drenching my words is more than I can handle. "Enzo, I..." I lift my gaze to his. Concern is etched on his face.

"Get the fucking doctor in here now," his order to Mario is filled with the same fear that's currently clogging my throat. The lump of emotion threatening to choke me is all-consuming. I can't do this. I can't lose one of the things that keeps me sane.

"I-I... This is..."

"Shh," Enzo coos, but I can't focus on anything other than the fact that my legs don't work. I can't move them. I can't feel anything in them. Not even pins and needles that come after being still for so long. "It's going to be okay. They'll fix it."

His words settle in my mind, but anger takes over and I pin my glare on him. "Fix it? This isn't something you can *fix*, Enzo." He stays silent, and I continue. "You can't just pay someone or threaten someone with their life and expect them to make me feel my legs again."

"I know, Luna," he whispers into my hair as he holds me close. I don't fight him. Not right now. My heart is slowly shattering into a million pieces and the only thing holding me together is the man I'm meant to walk down the aisle with, in a few weeks.

"What if I can't dance again?" I croak out. "What if I can't walk down the aisle?" Questions dance in my mind, taunting me as I attempt to consider my future.

The doctor walks in before Enzo can respond. I take the man in. He looks to be in his forties perhaps. Dark hair with a smattering of silver, small round spectacles, and a white coat. *Has he come to lock me up in a padded room, or tell me my diagnosis?*

"Ms. Cavallone," he greets, his gaze flitting between me and the bloodied man standing beside me. The doctor clears his throat. "I'm doctor

271

Peterson, and I'll be taking care of you while you're here. I've had a look at your charts, and I know you're concerned about the feeling in your legs. At this point, we will need to do more—"

Enzo releases me, rounds the bed and is in the doctor's face before he can continue. "You run every fucking test there is and you make her well again," he hisses. The doctor looks as shell shocked at the outburst as I am.

"Y-y-yes, of course, Mr. De Rossi," he says easily. But the stutter is apparent, the fear in his gaze is enough to make me shiver.

"Fix this," Enzo says once more.

Weariness overtakes me and I have to fight to keep my eyes open. "Doctor, please do the tests."

"I'll set it all up now. But you need to rest," Dr. Peterson says before leaving us. With Enzo needing medical attention, I'm sure they'll be busy for a while.

He comes to me, leans over, and presses his lips to mine. "It's going to be okay," he says confidently. Once they're gone, I lie back and allow the tears I'd been holding back to fall. They trickle as the pain of what I could face slams right into my chest, stealing my breath.

I just don't know if it is going to be okay.

LUNA

Panic.

It's all I feel.

It's as if I'm being held down, being pushed underwater, and my lungs struggle to work. There isn't a moment in my life that I didn't believe I would dance. Since I was a child, ballet has been my life, it's meant more to me than anything else, and now, it may be something I have to give up.

Enzo walks into the room, showered and bandaged, but I don't want to see him. Anger still grips my chest, and when he touches me, I flinch. I've never feared him, and even now, I'm not, but I can't have his hands on me. The reminder of his passionate kisses, how he made me feel, it's all been diminished by the fact that I'm broken.

"Luna," he coos my name as if it were a prayer. It's not. For him, I'll always be a burden. That's what I believe, and nothing can change my mind. There isn't anything Enzo says that will make me feel any differently.

"Please leave," I beg. It's been two days since the doctors have been working tirelessly to come up with some solution. Dr. Peterson told me it's a waiting game. It's only been fifty-two hours since the crash, and that's not enough time to confirm I'll never walk again. They've done scans and found nothing serious. I was told it may have just been the shock of impact that may have temporarily paralyzed me.

"Luna, listen to me. I'm—"

I turn to look at Enzo, my glare forces his words to a halt. "I said, get the fuck out of my room. I want to be alone." Enzo, the man who runs a mafia family flinches at my words. When I was first brought to him, I wanted to hurt him, to make him feel my pain, and I think, I've finally done it.

Silently, he nods, lowering his head, he turns and walks of my room, closing the door behind him. I'm finally alone again and I can wallow in self-pity. It's not fair for me to ask Enzo to stay with me. He needs someone who can do things for him. Not someone who will become more of a tiresome chore.

When the door opens again, it's not Enzo, but

Dr. Peterson. "Ms. Cavallone," he greets. "I have some good news. Or rather, better news." He stops beside my bed, the clipboard in his hand must hold answers because he's actually smiling. "The results of the latest scan show some bruising on the spine. That can lead to the paralysis you're experiencing. I've spoken with a colleague who's an expert in the field, and we'd like to operate."

His words sink in slowly. It's as if my brain is fogged up with information, too much information, and I can't work out what to say to that. I've seen enough movies to know that operations don't always help. But then again, when is real life like fiction.

"And this could fix whatever is wrong?" I ask, my voice weak with fear and exhaustion. I haven't been sleeping, mainly because each time I do, the nightmares attack and I'm woken with a start, my heart pounding in my chest and my head throbbing.

"We hope so. Dr. Hansen is confident that this will work," he tells me. "He's worked on many patients in the past with astounding results." He sets down paperwork on the small table and swings it over my bed. "I need you to look through these documents, and if you're ready to consent to the procedure, we can get you booked in immediately."

"Thank you, doctor." It's a whisper, my throat clogging with emotion. If my dad was here right now, he would've taken the lead. He would've read through this and chosen the way forward. But he's no longer here, and it's time I make decisions myself.

Dr. Peterson stops right at the door, glances over his shoulder and smiles at me. "The sooner we do this the better, Luna. The longer you're like that, the more difficult it could be to fix." His voice is tender, affectionate almost, and I'm close to tears.

All I can manage is a nod before he leaves.

I glance at the pages that he's left, but the words blur in front of me. I blink, allowing the tears to fall. Emotion trickles down my cheeks in rivulets of pain and agony. But it's not physical, it's emotional. I'm numb otherwise.

"Hey." I glance up to find Mario at the threshold of my room. "I thought you may need some company," he tells me as he steps inside and shuts the door, making his way to the bed. He stops beside me, offering a smile. "I saw the doctor leave."

I nod, and more tears fall. Mario reaches out gently, his thumb swiping at the wetness on my cheeks.

"I have to make a decision. He said it needs to be quick though." I don't recognize my voice. It's so broken, so defeated, even though the doctor said there is hope.

"Do you need help?" Mario asks causing me to look down at the pages, then up at him.

With a slow nod, I agree. He picks up the information and scans it with interest. "Okay, so this is an explanation on what they'll do." He sounds so confident; I wish deep down that I could feel that right now. "The bruising is on your spine, but they want to be sure nothing is fractured. From the scans, it doesn't look like it."

"A-and I'll be okay?" I sound like a child. Too young to be going through this. Too young to be hurting, to be losing ability to do something I love. It's selfish and arrogant, but right now, I don't care that I feel this way.

"It looks like it. Basically, the bruising should heal. It does take some time. But I think they want to rush the operation, so they know for sure that there aren't any nerves damaged."

"If there are?" I lift my gaze to meet his. Those eyes that have watched me over the time I've been in their presence hold warmth.

"There won't be," he tells me earnestly, but he can't know that for sure. Nobody can. Not until I consent and have professionals do their job. To have the doctors cut me open and make sure I'll be able to walk again.

"I sent him away," I admit once Mario sets the pages down on the small table once more. "I'm not angry at him, I'm..."

"It's not an easy thing to go through," he says.

"When you feel as if your life is about to change so drastically, it's difficult to comprehend. For anyone." Mario takes my hand, lifting my knuckles to his lips. He presses a soft kiss to them before he smiles. "Enzo isn't going anywhere. No matter how many times you send him away. The man is as stubborn as a mule. I've known him his whole life, and once he's committed, he follows through."

"I think I've fallen in love with him," I confess, still unsure of how to navigate these feelings. It happened slowly, over the past weeks. And as we head closer to the wedding, I realize that I want this.

"I know you have." Mario chuckles when my mouth pops open at his words. "It's so clear to see. He has changed. At least, around you he's different. And it's refreshing to see him care about someone so much."

"I wanted to hate him, so much. Maybe, I'm weak. He is meant to be my enemy," I whisper as I lie back, realizing that everything I've ever known is changing. I agreed that I'm Enzo's and I don't regret it. He's taken my heart, he's claimed my body, and I finally feel...*happy.* "I should apologize to him."

Mario nods, as if he was expecting me to say those words. "I'll get him. He's been in the waiting room, pacing back and forth like a caged animal since you told him to leave."

This makes me smile, the first time I've allowed

myself to feel happy since the accident. I can't do this alone. "Thank you for being here."

"Where else would I be?" Mario challenges. "And you should sign this." He taps the document waiting for my consent. "We want you healthy and home." He makes his way out of the room and it's as if a weight has been lifted from my shoulders. There's a long road ahead, depending on what the outcome of the surgery will be, but with my new family by my side, I can make it.

The click of the door catches my attention, and there, on the threshold, waiting tentatively for me to say something, is the man I love.

ENZO

"Enzo," she whispers, and my heart stutters. It fucking stutters against my ribs before stalling for a second. My feet have a mind of their own as I rush to her. "I'm sorry."

"Don't you dare fucking apologize for being emotional," I whisper, my fingers brushing her hair out of her face. She's so beautiful. So fucking perfect, even here in a goddamned hospital bed. "I'm working on finding the bastard who did this."

"I just need you," she says, her voice soft, calm, and pained. "I have to make a decision. And it needs to be quick."

I nod slowly. "If it's to make you better, than I approve. I'll sign the damn thing, if need be," I tell her because it's true. I want her to dance again.

I know she can. There is no doubt that this girl is everything, she's far stronger than most of my men put together.

"I shouldn't have sent you away," Luna admits slowly, our hands interlocking, our fingers tangling. I lean in and press my lips to hers and tell her silently how much I love her. I haven't told her the words yet, I've been waiting for the right time, and perhaps this is it.

"Boss," Mario's voice comes from behind me. "We've found him."

"Bring him to the warehouse," I tell him, but keep my eyes on Luna. "Make sure he's secure. I'll be there within the hour." My girl's eyes are wide. She knows what's coming. There's no doubt in her mind that the man in question will be tortured while being questioned. But I already know who oversaw the hit on her. Tommaso's words to me had sealed my confidence in the fact that he ordered this bastard to kill Luna. And he will pay.

"Come back to me," Luna tells me as I pull the pen from my pocket, handing it to her which she accepts. I watch her sign the consent form. She's going into surgery while I go kill a man.

I won't be focused on him, only making him pay. And the thought of her having to go through this has the fire in my veins simmering. My thoughts are filled with what I'm going to do to him, while

I smile as his screams fill the warehouse. I'll make sure he sings sweetly for me, as I peel the skin from his body. Inch by fucking inch.

"All you need to worry about is coming home to *me*," I tell Luna when she hands me back the pen. I take her hands in mine, our fingers tangling together. For the first time in my life, my dead heart awakens, filling with an emotion that scares the fuck out of me.

Allowing love in opens you up to pain.

It allows others to hurt you, to make your life hell.

But for her, I'll do it any day.

"I lo—"

"No." I press a finger to her lips. "You'll tell me that when I see you again." Tears sparkle in her pretty eyes, and I bask in the affection she holds for me. She's seen every part of me, the man, and the monster, and yet, she still wanted to admit she loves me.

But now is not the right time.

I'm about to speak again when the doctor enters the room. "Ms. Cavallone," he says, stopping at the foot end of the bed. "Have you decided?"

Luna nods. "Yes, let's do it. I have to try." The pain in her words lances me, deeper than I could ever have expected.

"Great," the doctor says. "I'll get you booked in

urgently."

I turn to the man. "I need to take care of some business, but I'll be back as soon as I can. I trust you'll take care of my girl." My words cause him to blanche because there is an underlying threat in them. If he doesn't take care of Luna, I'll be taking care of him. And it won't be pretty.

"Yes, of course, Mr. De Rossi," he mumbles, fear obvious in his response. "Let me get this done and we can get you into surgery as soon as this afternoon," he says to Luna.

"Thank you." Luna's voice is a whisper, and I can feel her eyes on me, boring into me with frustration. When I turn to her, she rolls her eyes. "You don't have to threaten everyone in my life you know."

"When it means life or death, I most certainly fucking do," I inform her easily. "I need to go, but I'll be back before you come out of surgery." Once again, I steal her lips, parting them with my tongue to taste her sweetness. She's warm, her tears have trickled down her cheeks, wetting my face. When I finally pull away, I lock my gaze on hers. "You're going to be fine," I promise, *because if anything happens to you, I'll burn the fucking world down.* I don't voice my words, but I know it's clear in my eyes what I mean.

"I'll see you later," she tells me and then, I know I need to go. My blood already boiling at the thought of coming face to face with the man who tried to kill her. The man who hurt her. Vengeance rings in my ears as I make my way down to the car where Thiago is waiting.

"Mario's already at the warehouse, they're waiting," he tells me as we slip into the car.

My thoughts are at war. With me stepping into my father's shoes so quickly it's forced me into a role I wasn't yet ready for. I thought I was, but everything that's happened since his death has felt like I've been on autopilot.

Now, with Luna's surgery looming, I have come to learn that I'm in love. The thought of losing her confirms it. My father once told me when that emotion has settled in your soul, the idea of not having that person around you, it breaks you. It squeezes every ounce of emotion from your heart. And with her, that's exactly what it feels like.

As the car pulls up to the warehouse, and we come to a stop, Thiago kills the engine and glances at me in the rearview mirror. "Are you ready, boss?"

"I've been ready since I heard she'd been in an accident," I inform him. "Let's go." We exit the vehicle and make our way into the large, mostly empty warehouse. Inside, Mario along with a couple of our soldiers stand guard. A man once again is in my hot seat. When my father first introduced me to this place, I knew it would become my second home.

"It seems we found ourselves a coward," I say as I near the chair. The man in question looks so much older now than he did when we signed the contract. Even though not much time has passed. "Mario, why don't you tell me about our friend here?"

"Well, his name is Tommaso Cavallone. He hires men to do underhanded jobs for a fee," Mario speaks slowly as he circles the assassin who's bound with chains to the chair. Even though his struggles are futile, and he knows it, he doesn't stop. "He's fifty-eight, a Sagittarius, and he loves to drink a neat vodka after every kill." A chuckle vibrates through Mario's chest when Tommaso stills all movement, shock evident on his face when he realizes we've dug deep.

I arch a brow, my gaze meeting my best friend's before I ask, "Anything else I should know?"

"Yes, actually." Mario stops in front of me, but his stare doesn't leave our captive. "He likes to pay for entertainment, even when they're not legal." At those words, I can't help but feel my blood boil.

My hands fist at my sides before I nudge my head at the soldiers who await instruction. "Let's get him up on the pulley," I tell them while regarding the man who seems to know his time is up. "Oh, and take that cloth from his mouth, I'd like to hear his side of the story."

He's freed, dragged toward the metal cuffs that

hang from the ceiling. Once he's bound tight, one of the men tugs the filthy material from Tommaso's mouth.

"You're a fucking bastard! I will kill you!"

I laugh out loud at his curses. "Empty threats mean nothing to me, Mr. Cavallone," I tell him easily before pulling out my blade. My trusty weapon. My fingers fit perfectly around the handle. "Get him naked." Another order which is obeyed by my men. Once I'm happy with what I have before me, I step forward to start my most artistic kill yet.

ENZO

"So," I start, "Tell me about the most recent job you hired a hitman to complete. Oh, and by the way, the man in question will be dead very fucking soon."

"Fuck you," he spits, anger and venom lacing his tone, but I don't even flinch. I've spent my life finding men like him, binding them to the chair, or hanging them from the fucking ceiling. And I've killed them all.

"I don't deal well with people who don't respect me," I inform him, stopping inches from where he's bound, hands above his head, ankles in thick metal cuffs that spread his legs just enough for me to slide a blade where he may not want it. But that would tarnish this beautiful weapon. "Mario, bring me the items," I request, keeping my voice neutral, calm.

He doesn't know what he's about to experience.

Mario hands me the two items—a blow torch, and a pair of tongs.

"I think you are a man who would've been willing to save his own skin. So to speak," I continue talking to Tommaso as I flick on the torch. A soft hiss escapes the barrel along with a blue flame which hisses as it continues to burn.

"What the fuck are you doing?" he asks. His eyes widen when I lift my hand, the flame spitting at him inches from his face. Even though he tries to cower away, he can't. I lean in, bringing my sneer closer as I allow the blue to dance along his cheek. The scream that erupts from his mouth is like a symphony.

The stench of cooking flesh invades my nostrils, and all I can picture is my little dancer, lying in that bed, fearful for her future. I torch the left-side of Tommaso's wrinkled face, from his eye which is nearly popping out of its socket, down to his chin. When I pull the torch away, I watch the bubbling of his skin.

"What you did to my fiancée, I didn't like it, Mr. Cavallone," I inform him coolly. Picking up the metal tongs, I slide the smooth part of it against the wound I've inflicted to cause as much agony as I can. And then, I grasp the melted flesh between the tips and tug harshly, ripping skin from muscle and bone.

Tommaso's words are nothing more than babbles of a man who knows he's about to die. But I can't rush this because he needs to *feel* everything that I do to him. Mario injects him with a shot of adrenaline to keep him awake as his one eye flutters closed.

"I'm a very patient man, Mr. Cavallone." I set the tongs down and pick up my torch once more. This time, I crouch down before turning on the blue flame once more. It's such a beautiful color. A perfect hue which is so unassuming. It's dangerous, deadly, but it's also the color of a new day, a serene sky with the sun shimmering with promise. "Did you know that the true color of fire is actually blue?" I ask him before I continue my handiwork on his shins, until I see bone. Then, I move up to his thighs, getting impossibly close to the flaccid cock hanging at his crotch.

I rise just before his body gives up and he releases a stream of urine which splatters on the cold concrete below. Thankfully I step out of the way in time. I've become accustomed to victims doing that. Each time it happens, I'm not surprised. My first was enough of a lesson for me to watch for the signs.

"It seems you've had a little accident," I taunt, before I grab the tongs again, clipping them together to warn him of what's to come. When I thought about Luna on the way here, I knew I needed to make this man pay. But the need for vengeance has overtaken me more than ever before.

"P-please," he sputters. "I-I-I need-d t-t-the f-f-family to b-be mine." I can make out his words just enough to catch his explanation, but that doesn't mean shit to me.

I continue my task by gripping his flesh between the metal teeth and tugging it slowly from his body. He won't last much longer, and I know I should just kill him. But it's too much fun to hear him begging for mercy.

The chains clink as his body shudders. The agonizing grunts bounce off the walls of the warehouse as he's slowly drained of his blood and his life. I watch, my arms folded across my chest as the man who tried to kill my girl struggles to take in breaths.

I don't know how long I've been standing here, but the moment the light in his eyes goes out, I find myself smiling. Mario is at my side, Thiago on the other, with the two soldiers having a smoke as they watch the show.

For us, this is life.

For my girl, it will soon be her family who will protect her.

And for our future, I'm going to have to decide what we'll do once she's home. I want to move back into my childhood home. But to do that, it needs an overhaul. I glance over my shoulder at Mario. "Call the decorator," I tell him. "I want the De Rossi estate redone. I want a dance studio, a music room, and a library."

"Will do," he answers with a slight curve of his mouth. He knew I'd fall. But I don't know if he realized his conversation with Luna when they first met had perhaps nudged her feelings toward me.

We did have our fights.

She's tasted my blade a few times, but she never ran.

And that's what means more to me than she'll ever know.

By the time I'm back at the hospital, showered and changed, Luna is still in surgery. Night has fallen, and my anxiety is through the roof. I haven't seen either of her doctors yet, and that's only making me more nervous.

Mario joins me, settling in as we wait. My leg jumps as I count down the ticking of the clock which hangs against the sterile white walls. The stench of flesh is still in my nose, but satisfaction thrums through my veins. If Luna was home, I would've made my way straight there and fucked her in every room in my home. And then, I'd take her into the shower before making her come on my cock, over and over until she couldn't think straight.

"She'll be okay," Mario says, his voice low, just loud enough for me to hear. "She's a strong girl. Also, I think she quite likes to give you grief, so she'll fight this."

I can't help but laugh because he's right. She is strong. More so than I ever gave her credit for. There were times I thought she would break. At first, I wanted her to break, but then I noticed something else, her fire made me want to see more of that. And in the end, I craved her for the strong, assertive little minx she is.

"She will," I agree with a nod. "But there's a niggling of doubt that's fucking with my head, no matter how much I try to ignore it. You know?" I glance at Mario. He's been with me for so long, my sturdy rock, my best friend. I cannot imagine being able to run this family without him. "I want your brother to join us," I tell him then. "You're my blood, and so is he. Once he's finished his studies at Black Hollow, I want him in New York where we both can watch over him."

Mario's mouth drops open before he shuts it, and I don't miss the surprise on his face. "Are you sure? I just... I spoke to him and he's enjoying his time at the school. Made friends."

"Friends?" I arch a brow. "Is he hanging out

with Judah and Jordan Venier?" The brothers are going to be taking over the school soon. Judah, the eldest is in his last year of school, graduating with flying colors. Their father and mine have been friends for many years. The small town in southern Italy has brought many men into the life, and when the Venier brothers step into their roles, that school will never be the same."

"Yeah," Mario says, grinning because he knows that they're as bad as he and I were when we were there. "I can't stop him, but at least they're responsible for the shit they cause."

"Not like us?" I challenge, shoving him in the shoulder. I miss the days when life was simple. When I didn't have an army to wield and a woman to marry. But when I hear the doors to the operating room slide open, I realize it's not true, because I would never change the moment that I rise to my feet to see Doctor Peterson walking toward me with a small smile on his face.

"Mr. De Rossi," he greets.

"Is she okay? Can I see her? What's the prognosis?" The questions fall from my mouth with a breath. My heart is banging against my ribs painfully as he looks at me then Mario before meeting my questioning gaze.

"The surgery went well," he tells me, and I let out the breath I'd been holding. "There was a little bruising as we suspected, but nothing serious. She'll need time to heal, but give or take a few weeks, she'll be able to start physical therapy. The paralysis is likely a temporary reaction to the crash."

Another breath expels from me and relief washes through my veins. Mario's hand on my shoulder squeezes in solidarity. He's come to care for her as well, and I don't blame him. At least I know if anything were to ever happen to me, she'll be safe.

"Thank you, doctor."

" She's in recovery now. She'll be out for another few hours, but you'll be able to go in and sit with her," the man informs me, before he offers his hand, and we shake on it. Once he's gone, I flop back into the chair and drop my head, my focus on the ceiling as my stomach unknots itself.

"Told you she'll get through this," Mario says, and I can hear the smile without looking at his face. The white of the walls are no longer stark and cold, but offer a promise, just like the bright blue sky on a warm summer's day.

"We have a wedding to plan," I tell him, before we both laugh out loud, and I pull my phone from my pocket to send an email. Life is about to change once more. And I want to be prepared for it.

A new home.

A beautiful wife.

A family that means more to me than I could ever have imagined.

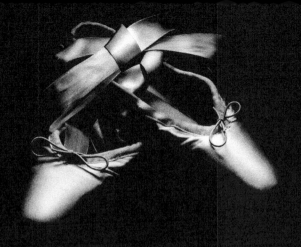

LUNA

Two weeks later

I'M STILL SORE WHEN I MOVE, BUT THE TINGLING HAS come back into my legs, reminding me that I'm alive. I've never been more thankful for the men in my life—the two doctors who made sure that I'll be able to dance again.

But more importantly, when I opened my eyes and saw Enzo waiting for me at my bedside, my heart swelled with emotion. My throat clogged up and I couldn't speak for a long while as he professed the things that he did to my uncle and the man who hurt me.

It turns out my uncle hired someone to kill me. And even though it shouldn't hurt because I knew he was a bad person, it still stung that someone I grew up around wanted me gone forever. All because he had so much hate in his heart, he couldn't think straight.

The warmth of the sun bathes me in its golden light as a gentle breeze sweeps through the bedroom. For a moment, I think of my mother and what she would make of everything I've been through. Perhaps she's looking down at me right now. But I no longer believe in heaven and hell because I've seen things that would make me believe hell is on earth with devil's walking around, running clans and organizations.

My bedroom door opens, and the nurse that Enzo hired comes in with a tray of breakfast. He's been home every day since I got home. It's been two weeks since I opened my eyes in the hospital bed and found him in the chair, his eyes locked on me.

"Thank you," I say to her as she sets down the food, and my stomach rumbles in response to the delicious smells.

"Today, the doctor will be doing a checkup," she tells me. "You're doing really well, so we foresee you walking normally in a couple of weeks of therapy at the minimum."

"I can't wait to dance again." My body has been healing, and with every step I take, I know it's in the direction back to the studio. I've been focused because I have to get back to doing what I love. And I also need to be able to walk down the aisle.

"You will," she assures me with a smile. "I spoke with Dr. Peterson, and he did say as long as you continue your daily walks, massages, and rest, you'll be able to get back to normal soon."

She bids me a farewell and I dig into the buttery toast on my plate. I close my eyes and savor the savory goodness before picking up my cup of green tea. I've always loved the taste, but I remember how Dad would scrunch his nose when he took sips just to annoy me.

"You look like an angel lying there," Enzo's voice drags me from my memories, and I smile when I see him in casual clothes. The man in a suit is mouthwatering, but when he's relaxed in a pair of gray sweats and a black tank, it's even more breathtaking than I could ever have imagined.

"And you look like you're not going to work," I remark, ogling him from head to toe and back again. He's barefoot as he pads to the bed to press a kiss to my forehead. He wanted me in his bed when we arrived home, but the doctor said it would be best if I had space, and that I shouldn't be disturbed. That brought a blush to my cheeks because it was clear what he meant by that comment.

"I'm going to be practicing with you today," Enzo tells me before stealing my lips with his. His tongue darts into my mouth and we tangle together in a passionate kiss that has my toes curling with pleasure.

I've missed him.

I've been frustrated that we can't do anything, but I know it's not going to be long now.

When Enzo pulls away, I catch the grin on his face because he knows what his kisses do to me. He enjoys taunting and teasing until I'm begging and pleading.

"You're going to therapy with me?" I ask, changing the subject before we can get lured into topics that will only distract me from what I need to focus on.

"Yes." He settles on the bed and grabs a grape, before popping it in his mouth. Happiness warms my chest and I finish my breakfast and allow Enzo to help me get out of bed. He leads me into the adjoining bathroom. Even though I would usually like privacy, having him with me is a relief.

Also, the day after I returned home, he refused to let me be alone for twenty-four hours. The man is a pain in the ass to get rid of, but I love how attentive he is. Being in pain, not having the strength to do certain things alone is frustrating, but Enzo has been by my side through it all.

I recall a conversation we had the second night of me being home.

"I never wanted to be a burden on you," I tell him.

"Like fuck you are," he grits through clenched teeth. His frustration is evident. "You're mine, Luna, and I told you, I'm not walking away, and neither are you."

"Well, I physically can't," I tease, hoping to lighten the mood, but the glower he pins me with has me shrinking back on the bed. Enzo leans in, his face inches from mine and his hand wraps around my throat. I can't deny my body as it responds to his rough touch. Even the pain diminishes when all I see, all I feel is him.

He locks those dark orbs on mine, focused, confident, and commanding. He holds my attention like he's gripping my neck. "You can never leave me."

"What makes you think I won't?" I sass him easily.

"Because the moment you do, I'll hunt you down, drag you back to my house, and tie you to my bed." There's no lie in his words. It's a vow. A promise. I started out as his enemy, and now, I've become someone he cherishes. Someone he really loves.

"Understood." I play coy, but he knows I'll continue to challenge him, and when I'm all healed, he's going to have his hands full. That's my promise.

When I'm done, Enzo helps me into the bedroom where I change into a pair of loose-fitting pants and a fitted tee. We make our way to the studio where we've been doing our walking exercises for the past couple of weeks.

Dr. Peterson along with the physical therapist, Elisa, are standing near the door waiting for us. It's my doctor who smiles and speaks first. "You're looking good, Luna," he says. "I was just telling Elisa you'll be back to your usual self in a couple of weeks. The only thing we need to watch is your dancing. I don't want you doing any jumping, or anything that could put a strain on your back yet."

"Thank you, doctor." A smile curls my lips as relief washes over me. At least he didn't say I *can't* dance at all. And that's something. "So, I can do anything else?" I test, glancing at Enzo who I can tell wants to know as well. It's been too long, and I do miss him.

Dr. Peterson offers a knowing smile. "Don't tire her out, and don't let her do anything strenuous," he warns Enzo who only chuckles in response. I have a feeling I have an evening of pleasure coming, and I look forward to it. "I better get going. I'd like to see you in my office in the next couple of days for another checkup," he tells me.

"I'll be there. Thank you, doctor." Once he's gone, Enzo grabs my hand and leads me into the studio for my therapy, and I know that one day, he'll take my hand and lead me down the aisle.

EPILOGUE

LUNA

Two months later

EIGHT WEEKS AND NOTHING.

No ring.

No proposal.

And I'm on the edge of my seat.

I've been dancing every day but taking it easy. I've been feeling so much better, and the pain is mostly gone. There are still times I get a twinge, but I've been making the most of being able to move freely, and without Enzo holding me up.

The studio is filled with a soft yellow glow from the fairy lights I asked him to put up for me. He's surrounded the whole room with them, and it feels as if I'm in a fairy tale rather than my dance studio.

I flick on the stereo system and run through my playlist to find a song to dance to. I want to do something different today, so I hit play on Ramsey as she sings *"See You Bleed"*. With my eyes closed, I picture the studio and allow my feet to carry me through a routine. It's nothing special, but when the melody courses through my veins, it feels natural.

No choreography.

Just me.

Just the music.

I spin in a slow pirouette, lifting one leg to stretch into a split, and it feels good to trust my body again. Lowering my foot to the floor, I bend backward, and find no twinge of pain as I twist and turn on the ball of my left foot.

My arms stretch out behind me, as I look up at the ceiling. When I straighten once more, I tip my toe to the bar, and lift my heel to the cool metal pole. I lift my right hand to the ceiling, curving my arm as I lift onto the toes of my left foot. I do that a few times before the chorus hits, and I hear the clap of hands.

I snap my gaze to the door to find Enzo leaning against the door frame. He looks so good in a crisp white unbuttoned shirt. It hangs open, pulled from the confines of his belt. His black slacks hug his thighs, but he's barefoot which makes him seem rough, as if he's just been in a fight and he's ready to take advantage of me.

The thought makes my core pulse with the need to be filled. My cheeks heat as he pushes off the wall and stalks toward me. His slow approach has my heart thudding against my chest and my stomach twisting with need.

I move to lower my foot, but Enzo's dangerous tone stops me. "Don't. Stay just like that," he orders as he reaches me. I turn to regard him in the mirror, his reflection makes my skin tingle with awareness. The heat of him cocoons me, and his hands grip my hips.

"Enzo." His name is a whisper dripping with need.

"You look so pretty," he tells me, allowing his one hand to trail up my body before clasping his fingers around my throat. "But I like it better when you cry," he informs me in a husky drawl that has every inch of my body sparking with electricity.

His other hand releases my hip before gripping the flimsy material of my tights and he tugs until I hear the tear that rips the cloth from my body. Then, the familiar blade is against my skin, but even the cold metal doesn't cool my body as he trails it up between my breasts.

"Are you ready, little dancer?" he coos in my ear causing goose bumps to rise in the wake of his question. I nod. But Enzo isn't appeased. "Answer me," he growls in my ear this time making me whimper with need. His fingers tighten around my neck, and he tugs me flush against him. My ass against the hardness of his cock.

"Yes, Enzo," I whisper, and then he slowly slices down my middle, the top I'm wearing falling away and baring my tits to him. My pussy is dripping as the next song comes on. The dark, thumping beat of Zolita fills the room as she sings, *"Hurt Me Harder"*.

The corner of Enzo's mouth quirks as if he's also listening to the lyrics. His hand shifts and he nicks the soft skin above my belly button. He tips his thumb against the small wound and brings it to his lips. "Perfectly fucking delicious," he whispers against my cheek before he steps back leaving me shivering at his absence. "I'm going to fuck you just like that, little dancer. Don't move." His words send lust thrumming through my veins.

The hiss of his zipper is loud above the music, but perhaps that's because my senses are on alert. The heavy bass of Sickick's *"Kill Me Slowly"* comes through the speaks, and I'm about to speak when Enzo thrusts into me in one feral push and I'm filled to the hilt with his thick, hard cock.

"Oh god!" My voice is shrill, but he doesn't stop. His hips move back before slamming against my ass, my one leg still up on the beam as he uses me for his pleasure. But that's not like him because his hands trail to my front, one grips my neck and the other taunts my clit until the one knee I'm trying to hold up starts shaking as my release nears the precipice.

My eyes shutter, but Enzo's grip tightens. "Watch us," he orders, the command doesn't leave room for debate, and I fight to focus on our reflection. I look like a rag doll being taken and used, and I love how feral and animalistic Enzo looks as he drives his cock deep inside me.

I'm so close.

He throbs inside me while I pulse around him, and as the music comes to an end, Enzo pinches my clit until I see stars, and I scream my release into the quiet of the studio. It doesn't take long for him to empty himself inside me, and the warmth of him has me shuddering through another orgasm.

He helps me to stand, because I'm weak from the euphoria shattering me, but his arms are wrapped around me as if I were made to be there. We lower to the floor gently, with Enzo's lips against my forehead.

"I want to talk to you," he whispers, and I have to flutter my lashes to look up at him.

"Now?" My incredulous tone makes him chuckle.

He nods, bringing me in for a soft kiss before he lifts me into his lap and I'm sitting on his expensive tailored slacks dripping with our release, but he doesn't seem to care. "I should do this properly, but our lives aren't perfect." His words settle in my heart, right down into my soul and I smile. "So, in the vein of being imperfect, in the same mindset of you being nothing more than a damn obsession for me in the beginning, I'd like to change that."

I arch an eyebrow at his affectionate, yet amusing proclamation. "Oh?"

"I want you to be my queen," he says confidently. "I want you to stand beside me in this world filled with violence, torture, and at times, death. But mostly, I want you to grow old with me. I've never once wanted to have a woman in my bed every single night and every morning when I wake up."

"And you say you want me there?" I challenge. Even though it's been months, and I have slept in his room, it's always been *his*, not ours.

"I love you, Luna. I love you more than I can breathe sometimes, and it scares the fuck out of me, but I want you to scare me forever." My throat clogs with emotion at his admission, and I blink as tears escape my lashes and trickle down my cheeks.

"I love you too, Enzo," I finally confess. It's been sitting on my tongue for so long, but I never felt like it was the right time.

"Then perhaps I should take you to our bedroom and show you again just how much I fucking love you," he says, and we struggle to stand. His hand tangles with mine as he leads me to the room which he caught me snooping in on my first day here.

When we step inside, I take in the change. The black and charcoal color scheme is still there, but he's added a myriad of fairy lights all over the ceiling as if we were looking up at stars.

"For you, my queen," he says before dropping to one knee and pulling a box from his pocket. When he flicks the lid, I gasp at the beautifully designed ring—a white gold band with a princess cut diamond surrounded by small sapphires.

"Oh my god, Enzo," I whisper as he takes it from the bed of velvet. Enzo takes my hand gently, before sliding the jewel on my finger. "I didn't say yes yet," I tease, and giggle when he glares up at me.

"Like I said, even if you run, I'll find you."

I don't doubt that. "Then yes, I'll be yours forever."

"Forever, my little dancer." And then he pulls me into his arms and leads me to our bed.

And I know forever is only the start.

My king and I will rule the kingdom together.

EPILOGUE

ENZO

One year later

I DIDN'T EXPECT TO HAVE THE LIFE I DO NOW.

My wife is walking beside me as we step off the private jet. She wanted to see Black Hollow, and I agreed. Mario joins us as we make our way to the waiting cars. The isle is small, you could probably drive from one end to the other in a couple of hours. Half the island is taken up by the school, Black Hollow Elite, and the other side is the estates and student accommodations.

Besides that, it's cut off from the mainland which makes it the perfect place for the young minds to focus on what's important—school. Yes, they do learn more than most normal schools teach, but the

311

focus is for them to get the education needed to run a clan, organization, Familia.

"This is beautiful," Luna says in awe as we drive through the forest from the airstrip making our way to the Venier estate. Only a handful of families own property on the island. A year ago, after Luna agreed to marry me, I knew I needed my full focus on the Familia, as well as my own growing family.

Instead of coming over to Black Hollow every six months, I met with Guida Venier or better known by his English name, Judah Venier, along with his father, and I offered them the option to buy my shares of the school. They accepted, and now, I'm merely a guest.

"This is one of the places that will always protect you. If you ever need help, call on the Venier's. Even though Judah is still young, he's trusted by my family." This is what I explain to Luna as we make our way up the driveway which leads to the mansion. The place is a palace, it overlooks pretty much half the island, and in the distance, the school can be seen from the windows of the house.

We exit the car once it comes to a stop, and I take Luna's hand. She looks like the queen I knew she was. Her black pants suit makes me want to hide her from hungry eyes, but I have to come to terms with the fact that my wife is a temptation.

The door to the house opens the moment we

step up onto the porch. "Mr. De Rossi," Judah grins as he opens the door, holding out his hand. He's in his early twenties, but he's been in this life for a long while now. His father wanted him to take over the school because he's young enough to understand the minds of the students, but also old enough to make informed decisions.

"Cut the crap," I tell him before pulling him for a one-armed hug. "How are you?"

"Living the life." He winks playfully before his gaze lands on Luna. "I knew you married a queen, but good lord," he remarks before taking Luna's hand and pressing a kiss to her knuckles which has me on edge.

"Okay, Venier," I warn, my tone no-nonsense, but the asshole just laughs. He's a playboy, enjoying the power and intrigue that comes with being Underboss. His status is well-known around the clans, and I know he uses it to his advantage to get women into his bed.

"Mario," Judah greets my right-hand man, ignoring my jealous outburst which I can only assume will be the same as the rest of our visit. "It's good to see you. Malachi is somewhere around here," he tells Mario.

"I hope we're not intruding on your college parties," I tell Judah.

"Not at all. My father was just here, he went

back to Italy this morning. It's good to have some friends visit as well. I'm sure you'll enjoy your time on the island."

"I look forward to seeing my brother," Mario says. I know he's been tense seeing Malachi again, and even though I've reassured him it will be fine, he's anxious. I don't blame him, but I wish he would trust in his brother's decisions. Even though we've given Kai as we nicknamed his brother, the choice to join the De Rossi clan, he's decided to stay at Black Hollow longer. There's nothing wrong with it, but I have a feeling Mario is going to have a tough time accepting that his brother is so far.

"Let's go," Judah says as he leads us up the stairs and down the hall. "This is your bedroom; I'll leave you to it. I need to head out and pick up a new student, but when I return, we'll have dinner."

"Thank you." I nod, shaking his hand once more before I'm left alone with Luna. She's been taking on more responsibility in the Familia, and I'm so fucking proud of her. "Here we are," I tell her.

"I love it. This is amazing," she turns to regard me with a small, shy smile. The same grin that captures my heart time and time again. "I need to speak to you about something." Her voice turns serious which makes my stomach drop.

"Is something wrong? Is it your back? Are you having—"

"Enzo," she calls my name, rushing to me and cupping my face in her soft, gentle hands. "Nothing is wrong," she says, her tone a whisper as he presses her lips to mine. Our gazes locked, and I note how utterly breathtaking she looks. "Are you ready to be Daddy Enzo?" she murmurs against my mouth and my whole world fades to just her.

"What?" I realize how harsh it sounded, but Luna only giggles in response.

She gives me a quick kiss before stepping back. "I'm pregnant, Enzo." For a long moment, I stand and stare at her stupefied. *A father? Me?* "Uhm, you kind of have to say something now." Her sass has held me hostage to this beauty since the moment she first spoke to me. And I know nothing will change as we grow old together.

I drop to my knees, and for the first time in my life, I shed tears. "Thank you," I croak as emotion chokes me. I pull her into my hold and press my ear against her stomach which isn't showing yet, but I pray to a God I never believed in, that our lives continue to be blessed. Just the way Luna came into my life to illuminate it with her light.

"Forever," she promises.

"Always." I agree.

THE END

Thank you so much for reading Twisted Obsession. If you enjoyed it, and you're wanting to dive into more dark deliciousness, The Devil's Plaything is a dark mafia romance that will definitely keep your Kindle steamy!

Keep reading for an excerpt of The Devil's Plaything…

VICTOR

Prologue

COLOMBIA.

My home.

My kingdom.

I was born to a father who would ensure his organization—running drugs—was known for the utmost quality, and that any shipment promised, would arrive on time. He could take a baseball bat to the face of the men who worked for him if they were caught stealing, and nobody would recognize them again. Importing drugs was what he did best, and nobody got away with theft. He knew every kilo and every ounce that was brought into the country, and he knew when it left.

He didn't feel guilt, shame, or any of those human emotions that make us weak. My father wasn't weak, and neither am I. He showed me the way, leading by example.

This is my life.

Before, the pressure wasn't on me. I could fly under the radar in my father's organization. Now, I'm the man who rules it all, after having taken over from papá, Luis Cordero, who died a proud man, knowing that his life's work would live on through me. On his death bed, he told me he was ready to go because he knew I was ready. Now, everyone fears *me*. When I walk onto the street or into a building, hushed whispers follow me. I wouldn't have it any other way because when people are afraid of you, that fear will bring about some form of respect.

I learned that from my father. He gave me everything I own, and some things I took for myself. The one thing you need to know is I'm not apologetic in any way.

I don't ask, I don't beg, I take.

It doesn't matter what or who it is, if it catches my eye, I will own it.

The tug against my jacket—where I slipped my wallet into only twenty minutes ago when I was at the restaurant—and the mumbled words, *"rico maldito bastardo,"* ring in my ears as if it's a foghorn blaring in the dark night. I feel for it, realizing my wallet is no longer in my pocket, but the man who's attempted to steal from me doesn't make it far. One of my men grabs him by the scruff of his neck, dragging him back to where I'm standing at the market stall.

Ignoring the woman who's serving me the crisp, green apples, I turn to find the thief. He's nothing more than a vagrant who's running around on the streets. If he had come to me and asked for a job, I may have considered it, but he's tried to steal from me, and he's mouthed off.

Granted, he may be right, I am a *rich fucking bastard*, but I'm the only one who can say that about myself. Anyone else spews venom, or even if someone takes from me, disrespects me in some way, I'll make sure they pay with a pound of flesh or a gallon of blood. Either way, they'll learn from their mistake. And this is why I'm in the town center with my men flanking me.

"*Perdóneme*?" I smile as I watch two of my men force him to the ground. Silence falls around us, and I revel in the way I've captured the gazes of the people around the market square. I love to put on a show; most times, it's in the privacy of my home, but right now, I think they all need to see what I do to assholes like this.

Once he kneels, his mouth is forced open by,

one of my youngest men, Alejandro. I lean in, my gaze locked on his dark one. Reaching for a handful of red sand, I grasp the granules and drop the whole lot in his mouth. The spluttering is enough for me to ensure everyone's heard him, but it's not enough.

If he'd kept to merely insulting me, I may have considered mercy, but stealing is another thing altogether. I straighten and gesture for my men to grab his wrists and force the left one to the ground, making it easier to access.

"Please, don't do this," the voice of the man kneeling at my feet whispers as he peeks up at me. The plea for mercy evident in his gaze. His voice is raspy from the sand I shoved into his mouth only moments ago. I watch him choke and cough, and I smile.

My black shoes are no longer shiny; instead, they're covered in the dust that he's disturbed. The toe of my shoe presses harder on the thin, fragile wrist of his left arm. Alejandro passes me the heavy leather wallet, which is thick with notes, and I slip it back into the pocket the thief swiped it from.

"What you need to understand, heathen," I bite out, leaning closer, so he can hear me. I feel the crowd that gathers, their eyes on me as I make a spectacle of an asshole who decided to disrespect me in the middle of the street. It wasn't my plan, but this piece of garbage forced my hand, and now,

I'll take his. "I don't take kindly to having someone like you disrespect me. I work hard to give you what you need. And I certainly am a good boss to you. You, on the other hand," I smirk, shoving the metal harder into his flesh, breaking it and causing blood to seep from under my shoe, making the red sand turn a dark brown. "You don't deserve my mercy."

I reach for the blade that Javier hands me, and I slowly toy with the sharp tip of metal right at the inner wrist of the man who's still pleading with me. The deep crimson liquid seeps from the small cut. I twist the blade around and around, watching as the knife inches deeper into the wound.

It doesn't take long for the gash to widen, the metallic fluid to shoot from the veins that have severed. Thankfully, with the razor-sharp serrated edge, I can slice evenly into the bone, listening to it crack. Flesh spews from the open wound, his hand lies an inch from his arm and his face is contorted in pure anguish.

He writhes in agony, and his cries are music to my ears as I rise. Pulling the handkerchief from my pocket, I wipe the blade clean and throw the small scrap of material on the asshole clutching his handless arm.

Turning, I meet the eyes of the people who live in the city I rule and tip my head in greeting before I turn away. I don't need to tell them what or why I did that, all they need to feel is fear.

For me.

Because I'm the King.

And everyone knows my name.

ONE CLICK NOW!

ALSO BY DANI

For a full list of Dani René's incredible titles visit
her website at www.danirene.com

ABOUT DANI

Dani is a *USA Today* Bestselling Author of seductive and deviant romance.

Her books range from the dark to emotional, but every hero is alpha, and each heroine is strong-willed, bringing the men down to their knees. She now lives in the UK, after moving from Cape Town, with her better half who does all the cooking while she writes all the words.

When she's not writing, she can be found binge-watching the latest TV series, or working on graphic design. She has a healthy addiction to reading, tattoos, coffee, and ice cream.

www.danirene.com | info@danirene.com
Or join her reader group on Facebook at Dani's Deviants

Printed in Great Britain
by Amazon

36803715R00192